CW00508717

THE CLAÍOMH SOLAIS

Declan Cosson

ISBN-13: 9781739369323
ISBN-10: 1477123456

Cover design by: Phillipe Cosson
Library of Congress Control Number: 2018675309
Printed in the United States of America

CONTENTS

"Where green is worn,
Are changed, changed utterly:
A terrible beauty is born."
- W.B. Yeats

PROLOGUE

A long time ago, before Christ was born, before Caesar marched on Rome and before Moses led the Israelites from bondage, there lay a small island at the edge of fair Europa, whose name was Ireland. According to legends of the distant past, Ireland was ruled by a race of beings known as the Tuatha De Danann. Tutored by the noble Goddess Danu, these people became her tribe. The world of these people was fuelled by magic which allowed them to carve out great cities and wield immense destructive power, they even created ships that could fly. It seemed at first that they had created a paradise on earth in Ireland. However, such wonders never last. The Tuatha De Danann were attacked by a race of monsters known as Fomorians.

At first the Tuatha De Danann were able to defeat the Fomorians, but their king, Nuada lost his arm, forcing him from the throne and plunging the tribe into a succession crisis after which the half Fomorian and half Danann prince, Brés, ruled Ireland with a tyrannical fist, forcing the Danann to work as slaves and making them pay tribute to the Fomorians. Brés' dark reign came to an end when another half Fomorian and half Danann prince, Lugh, the grandson of Balor himself, led the Tuatha De Danann in revolt. Brés turned to the Fomorian king Balor for aid. Balor gave Brés an army of giants, formed from metal and fuelled by magic which could only answer to Balor himself. This army helped the Fomorians almost completely obliterate the Tuatha De Danann until Lugh slew Balor. Balor's army collapsed, bringing the war to a halt.

However, the cost was so great that it weakened the Tuatha De Danann and their magic, allowing them to be defeated by the invading Milesians, or Celts as we would know them today who forced them into the mounds with fire and iron. While many of the tribe of Danu died out, some mingled with the new mortal humans that had conquered their territory, but this had the result of diluting their power and causing a catastrophic decline of their magical abilities to the point that their descendants while still having supernatural strength, were little more than mortal humans with long lifespans.

Centuries later, around the fall of Rome, King Brés tried to resurrect Balor so that he could conquer not just Ireland but all of Britannia as well. At that time, he was foiled by the Roman-Brythonic King Arthur, forcing Brés into hiding for more centuries. During that long time, Brés emerged as a leader of all the creatures of the night, hoping one day to conquer Ireland once again.

1

Digging for the Sword

It was the year 1944 and the sun was floating above Ireland while waves crashed against the rocky coast. Every so often, it was possible to see a whale leaping out of the sea only for the giant creature to come crashing back under the water and disappear below the surface. Although the sun shone down upon the land, the breeze from the Atlantic was chilly. This didn't stop an archaeological dig from taking place not too far from Killala. The dig site covered a vast area of the coast and surrounding the place was a large array of encampments. There was a dusty path that linked the camp to the main road. The site was busy and loud as up the path came two horse drawn carriages carrying men and a truck carrying equipment. Labourers hammered their way into the earth with pickaxes and spades. Many of the workers were sweating because of the long, arduous work.

One of these labourers was a boy of sixteen with hair as brown as oak. Aside from that, nothing made him stand out much from the other labourers. Feeling his arms sore from the digging, he paused to ask a question of one of his mates.

"Colm, what time is it?"

The labourer beside him looked at his watch.

"According to my watch, it's only a quarter past three, come on, keep digging!"

"Eh, remind me what we are digging for again? Something to do with a sword, right?"

Colm sighed.

"According to the boss, Damien, we're looking for a sword known as the "Claíomh Solais", one of the four treasures brought by the Tuatha De Danann to Ireland."

"What? The Tuatha De Danann? Aren't they a myth?"

"I couldn't give a rat's ass if they're a myth or not, I just like the boss for paying us more than the council ever did."

Saying that, Colm lifted his pickaxe and slammed into the ground, displacing more dirt. Looking up and taking some deep breaths, the younger digger, Damien, could see the towering, athletic and beardless figure that was their employer, Eric Trent. Eric Trent had a stern face and vibrant red hair, and his long coat billowed in the wind as he paced around the place, inspecting the diggers. Damien knew that Mr. Trent was an Englishman born of England's upper class, having heard his sophisticated and stern voice. Following him was a wolfhound with dark grey fur; the creature looked old but it still made for an imposing sight.

The fact that he had a wolfhound and that he didn't just sit down and drink tea while watching the dig was, to Damien's eyes at least, a sign that he was more than just another scholar from London. On the other hand, his physical prowess and regimented behaviour made Damien more nervous around him than he would be around other Englishmen. Mr. Trent watched his diggers like a hawk, only taking his eyes off them to look down at his watch so as to check the time. Calum McKeone, an overseer, approached him.

"Mr. McKeone, how is the dig going, is there any sign of the mound?"

"Not yet, but there are other issues that need our attention."

Eric raised his eyebrows.

"What issues?"

"May I speak to you in private, Mr. Trent?"

Eric beckoned to him.

Calum McKeone followed the Englishman to the central tent, the largest tent in the encampment. As he walked, Eric whistled to his wolfhound.

"Come on, Oisín, let's go."

The wolfhound followed his master but when Eric entered the central tent, he indicated to Oisín to stay outside.

Eric and Calum approached a table which had an Ordnance Survey map displayed upon it. Although Calum sat down, Eric remained standing.

"Mr. Trent, we're getting a lot of pressure from the Lord Mayor of Castlebar...he's not happy that you, an Englishman are digging up Irish artefacts..."

"Mr. McKeone, this dig site is providing the employment that these people need. I thought I had arranged everything with the Lord Mayor. Once I retrieved the sword, I would go back to Dublin and hand it over to the Irish National History Museum. Then I could go on to the next artefact. What has changed?"

"Well, you see, the Lord Mayor is also under pressure from the priests..."

Eric's eyes widened.

"The priests? Do they have to interfere with everything men do here? It's as if they run this country, for the state fears them, the police fear them. It's like being in a monastery, here."

"They fear that you will take the treasure to London, give it to the British war cabinet to use in the "Emergency" against the Nazis."

Eric sighed in frustration.

"But you know that I intend to dig up the sword and take it to Dublin, I literally just said that, and this is what you must say to the priests! I will not let superstition interfere with the dig, most of all, you will tell them that I will keep digging. Is that understood?"

Calum looked alarmed.

"I understand your devotion to the art of archaeology, but you sir, you are walking a very dangerous path."

Calum walked out of the tent to oversee the men as they

kept digging. Sitting down, Eric switched on a radio which beeped and made some noises for a while. Finally, the song "Stalin wasn't Stalin" filled the tent, as Eric poured himself a glass of wine and took out a cigarette to smoke. As he smoked, he continued to examine the ordnance survey map which displayed the land of county Mayo. The location of the dig site was signified by an X. Eric was feeling stressed out, for he had carried out this dig for a month, with little result. The fact that the authorities didn't want him here made things even worse for him.

That evening, the working day had ended and Eric sent his workers home so that they could go back to their families. On the other hand, he and some others, including Calum, stayed at the tents. Damien cycled back to a town that wasn't too far from the dig. As he cycled on the gravel road, he had to keep his eyes focused on the surface so he didn't have time to look at the electric poles, wooden poles that were linked by wire, which lined the road.

This town wasn't too special, it just consisted of houses, a pub, a few shops, a church and a central place in which to hold a market. More electric poles were dotted throughout the town. Still not a single car or bus was in sight, mostly just carts that would be drawn by a horse, for both oil and gas were being rationed. Living in such a primitive world made it difficult for Damien to imagine that only across the sea from Ireland, the most advanced war in history to that point was taking place. A war which many of his schoolmates had gone off to join.

He continued to cycle till he reached his house. As he approached their small little garden, he could see that his younger siblings were still playing outside.

As he brought the bike to a halt, the eldest child, Seosamh cried out in Gaelic.

"Look, it's Damien, he's back from the dig."

Overjoyed, they ran towards Damien as he stowed his bicycle. The twins, one boy Aidan and one girl Eileen, clung onto Damien's legs as if trying to embrace him. Feeling slightly embarrassed by this attention, he told them to take it easy. This didn't stop them from pelting him with excited questions.

"So how was the dig?"

"Exhausting! It was chilly by the coast but I sweated as if I was in the Sahara because of the work we were doing. The boss pays us well, but he keeps us hard at work."

"But isn't there a wolfhound, Damien?"

"There is, he was a big fella and the boss calls him "Oisín". It's quite a surprising name for a Sassenach to give his hound."

"But Damien, can't we go to the dig, is it fun?"

Damien sighed.

"Ah now, you'll need to ask our parent's permission before you go anywhere near that site. Besides, I seriously doubt our mam will let you leave her sight anyway."

The two developed disappointed faces as they protested.

"But…"

"But nothing, the boss said that no one was to enter that site if they were under the age of sixteen."

Damien opened the door, allowing the children to precede him into the house.

As he entered the hallway, Damien slowly took off his cap. He saw his mother waiting for him.

"You're late for dinner, what happened?" she remarked.

"The boss has us work for long hours, Mam, but on the bright side, he pays us well, we might finally be able to sustain more than mere subsistence."

Damien was too tired to continue talking and he could feel his tummy rumbling, so he followed his mother to the table.

◆ ◆ ◆

That night, after dinner, Damien headed into the sitting room and sat down by the warmth of the fireplace. He looked for a while as the flames glowed and blazed, burning through the logs. His father, Donal, was sitting on the other side of the fireplace. If there was a way to describe Donal's father, it was a man that was not just drained of youth, he looked as if he was totally drained of energy all the time. Yet he had played an active part in Ireland's violent history at the start of the century. A sense of disillusionment had settled on his hardened, bearded face. He looked over at his son.

"So, Damien, how was your first dig? I hear you are working for a Sassenach archaeologist now, is that right?"

Damien leaned over to Donal and took out several pound notes from his pocket and handed them to him.

"Look on the bright side, Dad, he may be a hard boss but he pays at least 20 pounds a day for the work we do. Also, I've finally found myself a job, after years of trying and failing to find one."

Donal sighed as he raised his mutilated right hand to stop Damien from handing the money over. His hand was an unsettling sight as every fingernail had been damaged beyond repair, and the hand itself looked like a claw, as if it was a corpse's hand.

"Damien, you know my hand wasn't always like this, don't you?"

"I know and I know who did that to you, but I assure you the boss isn't like them, even if he comes from the same country."

"Damien O'Laoghaire! He is an Englishman, he's only here till he finds what he's looking for. You can keep that money to yourself, I'm not taking money from the same race of men that mutilated my hand and left us to starve!"

Damien was shocked as Donal pushed the money back into Damien's hand. Then his shock turned to anger.

"Dad? This money can help the little ones get food into their bellies. This money is what sustains our house, our clothing and even my bike! What has our government ever done for this town? I tell ye what it has done, the government has rationed our gas, our petrol, our food and we can't even get sweets for the little ones anymore! Why? Because there's an "Emergency", so I tell ye Father, when a handsome stranger comes in and offers us jobs, of course we accept his offer! Why? Because he actually brings to this town what our government hasn't been bothered to do, and that is provide well-paid jobs for young fellas like me! He searches for the "Claíomh Solais", the Sword of Light, he…"

"Damien! Life isn't just about money! Now listen, young man you could have easily found yourself a job at the pub as I have or at the council! Have ye forgotten how many lads died for our freedom, have ye forgotten our great leaders who died so that we wouldn't have to live in fear. I got my hand destroyed so that youths such as yourself wouldn't have to live with the chance that the King's soldiers would evict ye…"

Hearing all of this talk, Damien rolled his eyes. He had heard it all before again and again.

"Freedom for what? Dad? Freedom to be left behind by the modern world. Freedom to be poor and to live on scraps as we did before the Famine? Your talk of heroes means nothing when your belly rumbles and you don't have a penny in your pocket. You ask me if I have forgotten our heroes of the rebellion, but I ask ye, have you forgotten our generation, Dad, have you lads forgotten your sons? You talk to us about responsibility but we don't have the means, we don't have enough jobs…"

"Left behind by the modern world? Well thank God for that, Damien, because the modern world is caught up in yet another war, if we weren't left behind by the modern world, we would have bombs being dropped onto our little town, would you want that?"

Damien sighed.

"No, if I'm going to sire children, then I want to be able to drive them to school, not send them walking with bare feet; I'd like to be able to give them proper gifts each Christmas. You know, that's the magic that having a proper job means, most of my mates have gone to America anyway, I might have done that too, at least, before the Englishman came along."

"Damien, please, you don't understand the English....I get it, you're angry at me, you're angry at De Valera and you are angry at the priests, all because you've been struggling to find a decent job...but let me tell ye, Damien, once the boss has found this sword, I can tell ye he will have no more use for ye and..."

Damien had heard enough. He stood up.

"Fine, I'll keep your warning in mind but it is clear that you know nothing of the boss. Also, England is what is standing between us and a Sadist who rules the continent. And at the same time, it still manages to provide both its lads and even its lassies with jobs. Goodnight Dad!"

Feeling remorse for having ranted at his son, Donal straightened up in his chair and called after him.

"Damien? Damien, please, please wait.... Damien, I....I didn't mean to..."

But Damien paid no attention leaving Donal slump back down onto the chair in shame and anguish. He could still remember the agony from the burns he received after his truck was set alight by anti-treaty forces all those years ago. He had been there at the landings of Waterford; he had seen Collins get killed at Beal na mBlath.

Out in the hall, Damien's mother, Sarah, was waiting for him.

"Damien...were ye arguing with your father again?"

Damien hated to see the sadness in her eyes.

"Mam, in his own head, he acts as if it's still 1921 and that the British are still the enemy. He doesn't understand that we have an English boss who treats our town better than the state ever did. I mean does he hate me?"

"Oh Damien, don't say that. He doesn't hate you, he never did; he's just worried about strangers coming in and offering the lads employment for a short period of time only to then leave them all in the lurch without jobs, alright?"

Damien sighed. Deep down he felt angry because he knew his parents might be right about this kind of job but still, he took out his pounds and handed her the money.

"Mam, could you please get something with this money, so that I know that the hours I spent working today weren't for nothing. Get something for the twins. The boss has offered us a reward if one of us finds the sword. Think of what that will bring? Goodnight, Mam."

Sarah smiled fondly at her son.

"You're a good lad. Goodnight, Damien."

2

Heading for the chamber

Damien slept in the same bedroom as his younger siblings. The twins were already fast asleep when he arrived in the room. Damien didn't even change or undress himself. For now, he just slumped down onto the bed, sitting there and thinking to himself about all that had just happened. In some ways he longed for the days when his father and himself didn't clash and confront each other. He knew that the source of their tension was their economic position and he hated the Free State even more for allowing that to happen. On the bed beside him sat Damien's brother, Seosamh. He was leafing through some sort of old and tattered magazine, looking for short stories to read.

"So, what will happen if the sword is found?"

"If the Claíomh Solais" is found, Seosamh, the labourer who finds the sword will be given a reward by the boss. What that reward is, I don't know."

Hearing the word "reward" caused Seosamh's heart to flare up with excitement.

"Well, isn't that obvious? He's a rich Englishman after all, the reward is probably money!"

"Seosamh, everyone else is asleep, keep your voice down or you'll get into trouble."

"But Damien, don't you get it, why don't we go to find the sword? Imagine the reward that Sassenach will pay, we'd be rich! We could go to New York or even Hollywood! There we could taste the best food, drink the best wines, drive the coolest cars, wear the finest suits and even sleep with the most beautiful women in the world. And I won't have to wash the dishes anymore, right?"

Damien's eyes widened and his jaw dropped at what his younger brother was saying. Seosamh persisted.

. "Think of it, Damien, we could go to the dig site and snatch that sword, right?"

"When?"

"Tonight, we head for the dig site while there is no other competition and even if the boss catches us, we'll have found what he wants, right?"

Damien was hesitant at first.

"Seosamh?? Do you really think we should be going out at this time of night?? Do you realize the trouble we could get into if we break the rules?"

"Yeah well, Damien, Dad doesn't earn much, how long will it before he loses his job? If that happens, we'll get evicted. This is Ireland, Damien, if we do follow the rules, we still get punished. Since that is the case, why not break the rules trying to make a fortune?"

Damien wanted to pound his fist against the bed; he wanted to row with Seosamh. But he was tired from the day's work. And though he lacked the self-indulgence of his younger brother, the idea of being rewarded by a man of affluence was too tempting for him to shrug off.

"Alright, here's how it will go: for now, we get ourselves some sleep. When it gets to twelve o'clock, we sneak out and go to the dig site and search for the sword, alright? Until we find it, we make no mention of this to anyone, especially Mam or Dad, alright?"

"Yes, I get it."

"Good, now let's get some sleep."

The clock struck midnight. Seosamh and Damien got up and as quietly as possible snuck out of the bedroom. The wooden boards of the house creaked and groaned as the two went down the stairs. As they went out the door, they grabbed their flat caps and Seosamh grabbed a lantern so as to provide some light. The town was only dimly lit due to the restrictions on electricity. Seosamh, despite having a scarf tightly wrapped around his neck felt chilly. He whispered to his brother.

"Wow, this land sure gives me the creeps at night."

"I know, but look on the bright side, we don't have routine visits from bomber planes like the Englishmen do."

"Yeah, all the more reason to go to America, no bombs, no poverty, just fancy parties."

The boys grabbed Damien's bicycle and cycled off into the night away from the relative safety of the town and into the darkness of the countryside. Above them, the moon was glowing like a spotlight while the trees blew in the wind. Seosamh couldn't help but feel as if his whole body was shivering because he felt as if the two were being watched by something. It always felt like that when you went into the night in Ireland.

They cycled till they reached the dig site. The site itself looked more ominous without the presence of men working there and the breeze of the ocean still blew across the headlands. The boys could even hear the waves crashing against the rocks. As they parked their bicycle, they could see an elegant-looking car coloured in a vibrant red parked near the encampment. Damien knew that this was the car of his boss, Mr. Trent so he didn't go near it but on the other hand, Seosamh was captivated and felt tempted to approach the vehicle. Seeing this, Damien grabbed him.

"Seosamh, come on, will ye?"

"But Damien, I've never seen a motorcar like that, have you?"

"Alright Seosamh, but remember what we are here for?"

"I know, oh, where are the tools?"

"Follow me."

The boys went to the truck where all the tools were. Damien kept his eyes on the sleeping wolfhound as he eased into the space as gently as possible. Seosamh held the lantern firmly in his hand while Damien took a spade. All around them, crows started to gather. These big coal black birds could barely be seen but they croaked their mouths off so they were loud enough to be heard for miles. Even the wolf hound stirred at the sound. The sight of so many crows left both boys unsettled.

"Eh, is this a bad sign? Crows were the creatures of the Morrigan, were they not?" Seosamh asked.

"Yes, they were..."

"Oh no, she's the goddess of death, that can't be good."

"It was your idea to come and dig here, so come on, there is no turning back."

The dig site itself was already worn by the repeated hammering away at the earth by workers during the day. Although the earth below him felt unstable, Damien persisted till he reached the centre of the place. Using what strength he had, Damien plunged his spade into the earth and yanked out soil while Seosamh observed him. Seosamh knelt down while shining the lantern on Damien's efforts, allowing his older brother to see what he was doing. For now, regardless of what happened, Damien kept digging even though his arms ached. He was so focused on his digging that he didn't even notice that the wolf hound was barking as loudly as possible. Then, Damien plunged the spade even deeper than he had before. When he yanked it out again, all of a sudden, the ground began to shake.

Deeply alarmed, Seosamh and Damien scrambled back from the area as the ground started to split open. The split revealed a stone staircase that went deep into the ground, deeper than their eyes could see. The sight of this left the lads speechless. Seosamh's mouth opened wide open while Damien turned to him and said under his breath. "Sweet Mary, mother of Christ, we've just found an entrance."

◆ ◆ ◆

Meanwhile, Eric was fast asleep in a sleeping bag in the central tent. He found himself in the middle of a strange dream, a dream that depicted some sort of battle where he could see from the perspective of a figure fighting with a spear, leading these super strong warriors into battle against strange and distorted creatures. The warrior with the spear looked a lot like him, even sharing his bright blue eyes and vibrant red hair. At that point, Eric woke up to the sound of barking. The barking got louder and louder indicating that the dog was getting closer. Curious, he roused himself as Oisín came inside.

"What? What's happened? It's midnight my boy..."

But Oisín continued to bark anxiously.

"Alright, calm down, sonny, just let me get dressed and we'll find out what is wrong."

The wolfhound waited patiently as Eric dressed quickly in his suit, long coat and fedora. He grabbed both a torch and a pistol. He then fitted a collar around Oisín and let the dog lead him on. As he came out of the tent, he could see Calum emerging as well. The crows were still surrounding the dig site. Unsettled by the crows, Calum called over to Eric.

"Mr. Trent? I saw two lads at the dig, I can't make them out! They might be thieves."

"What? Come on. Let us find out if that is true!"

Both men ran towards the dig site with guns brandished and torches shining. The wind rose, causing the men's long coats to billow in the wind.

The two boys were still dumbstruck by what they had found. The rising wind was so powerful that it blew out the lamp, plunging everything into darkness. Seosamh began to panic.

"Damien, the lamp's burnt out, are ye sure that we should take the risk of going in?"

"Did you not bring matches Seosamh?"

"Eh, oh no, I knew I forgot something…"

Damien was exasperated.

"You didn't bring matches? Did you not realize the lantern could blow out ye dumb eejit?"

"I thought the lantern would last, how did this wind come blowing all of a sudden? What's with all the crows? What have we done?"

"Look I don't know, maybe ask the boss?"

Suddenly, they heard loud barking and the darkness around them was driven out by torches gleaming. Seosamh and Damien looked over as Calum pointed a gun at them.

"Alright ye thieving gits, we've got ye now, leave or we'll call the guards!"

Eric showed up behind him with the barking wolfhound but then suddenly Oisín twitched his nostrils which led both men to pause. For it seemed that the hound recognised the smell of one of the boys.

Curious, Eric shined his own torch on Damien. Recognising Damien, he laughed.

"Wait a minute, Calum, that "thief" is one of our diggers, and I'll wager he's here for my reward."

Eric put his own gun back into his pocket while Calum lowered his. Eric spoke again.

"Well, come on, young gentleman, stand up. What is your name again?"

"Damien sir, Damien O'Laoghaire, I'm sixteen years of age and I was your latest recruit."

"Indeed, you are here for the sword are you not?"

"Yes sir, I learnt that you have offered a reward and my brother Seosamh and I wished the honour of claiming it. Is there really a reward, sir?"

But Eric was no longer listening. He was looking at the stairway going down into the earth. He gasped. Calum looked at him curiously.

"You okay, Mr. Trent?"

"The stairs, yes the stairs, it's the exact stairs that I saw in a dream…"

Eric turned to the boys and continued speaking in a strange voice.

"Young men, do you realize you may just have found the resting place of the "Claíomh Solais"?"

Damien summoned his courage.

"We….did? Permission to ask how you know that Mr. Trent?"

"A dream. Ever since I came to this country, I've been guided to this place. That's how I knew to set the dig site here. Come boys, let's find the sword, already you have three hundred pounds from my family treasury awaiting you two and your family…spend it well."

He turned to Calum, giving him Oisín's leash.

"Mr. McKeone, guard the entrance of this place. Look after Oisín and if we don't make it out, give the £300 reward to the O'Laoghaires as compensation. Is that clear?"

"Eh…yes…"

"Please Mr. McKeone, I need to trust you on this."

"Of course, you can, Mr. Trent."

Seosamh and Damien followed Eric down the stairs into the ancient complex that they had just discovered. Damien was starting to develop many questions in his mind about Eric. Who was he? Why was he here? How did he get these dreams which told him exactly where to look? Why did he look so unnaturally handsome and was he really from England? Also, what was with the wind and the crows? Seosamh, on the other hand, was too excited to notice anything special because he felt his mother wouldn't be able to punish him if he came home with three hundred pounds. However, there was more for the boys to worry about than crows, wind or their parents.

Little did they know but Calum had gone back to his tent. It was the only one with a telephone. Calum took the phone in his hand and spoke into it saying.

"Good evening my Lord Donacagh, I've come to tell you that Eric Trent has found the sword. He thinks that I'm on his side…"

"Nice job, I'll send some men to meet him, we won't let this Englishman get his hands one of our great treasures…good work, McKeone, you will be rewarded handsomely for this."

Calum put down the phone. Oisín was whining and pulling at his leash which Calum had tied to a chair. Untying him, Calum said, "Come on, you, we're going for a w…"

But Oisín wasn't waiting for anyone. The dog leaped away from him and ran off barking. Calum was scared, for he knew that if the dog was loud enough, he would potentially attract attention to what was going on.

Down in the ancient complex, the boys followed Eric through a dark corridor illuminated by his torch. He had also given Seosamh a torch to hold. Seosamh looked up in awe at the intricate beautiful faces that were carved into the ornately designed walls.

"Mr. Trent? Is this a Celtic site? Does it not look too advanced to be Celtic?"

"Celtic? Oh God no, young man, this place is far older than the Celts, in fact this place even comes from a time before the Bible was written. It was built by the Tribe of Danu, "The Tuatha De Danann" as your people call them to hide the sword of light from the "Milesians", that means your people by the way."

"So, you're telling us that the sword is really "An Claíomh Solais", there was an Irish newspaper named that, you know, it's one of the four treasures of Ireland, right?"

Eric chuckled.

"Yes, good to see you know your mythology, Lady Gregory would have been impressed."

Eric continued to lead the way. Statues of men in armour clasping lances and shields lined the walls. As the three maneuvered their way through the place, they could see more beautiful faces on the wall. Though the faces and statues carved into the wall seemed to be those of beautiful maidens, they gave the boys the creeps because they both had a feeling of being watched. Seosamh had the ugly feeling that something was going to jump out at them.

"Has anyone else ever seen this place, Mr. Trent?" Damien asked Eric.

"Not for millennia. Strongbow, the lord sent by William to rule Ireland, the Viking Kings of Dublin, Hugh O'Neill and even the man you all hate the most, Oliver Cromwell, sent armies to try and find this place. Not a single man was able to find it. For more than many centuries since the defeat of the Tuatha De Danann at the hand of the Milesians, men and armies have fought over this very island, yet until now, not a single man has ever entered this place."

Seosamh and Damien looked at each other in awe at this. Eventually the three reached a circular chamber. The walls were patterned with statues and faces. As they shone their torches, the three gasped as they saw what was at the centre.

At the centre was an ornate altar and sitting on this altar was one of the largest swords that Damien and Seosamh ever saw. This sword was a large broadsword that had an ornate hilt and silvery blade that was even bigger than the swords used by knights.

Eric spoke tersely.

"You two wait here and shine the torches on the altar so that I can see what I am doing."

"But does this not look too easy?"

"Damien, I am painfully aware that this place may be booby

trapped so you two are to run if you hear rumbling. Understood?"

"Eh yes, Mr. Trent."

For now, the boys watched as Eric approached the altar. Eric himself started to shiver as he slowly approached the sword. His heart began to pump but he maintained his discipline as he reached out his gloved hands towards the sword. As he did this, he got a closer look at the sword and saw that the blade was patterned with symbols of a language that Eric couldn't understand. Both boys looked anxiously as he took in deep breaths before finally grabbing onto the hilt of the sword and lifting it up. At first, he was overjoyed while the boys sighed in relief but then an ugly feeling of dread developed in all their hearts.

Eric had little time to admire his conquest as the ground began to shake and rumble underneath him. He backed away with dread from the altar while he had the sword clasped firmly in his hand. Nervous at what was happening all around them, He turned to the terrified boys.

"Run! Just get out of here and don't look back!"

The boys ran and Eric followed them. Suddenly all the beautiful faces retreated back into the walls as if operated by some sort of mechanism that had been triggered by the taking of the sword. Emerging in their place were dragon shaped demonic looking faces with their mouths wide open. The three were running hard as darts shot out of these mouths. The three had just escaped from the chamber as a huge slab of rock slammed shut behind them. As they ran back up the corridor, the statues started flinging their spears at them in an attempt to stop the team from escaping.

Although they managed to escape being stabbed or chopped up, Seosamh tripped and fell to the ground. Feeling a great pain in his ankle, he tried to stand up only to quickly lose his balance. Desperate and terrified, Seosamh cried.

"Hey, wait up! Wait up, I can't make it, help!!"

Looking upwards he saw a slab descending towards him.

"Oh, sweet Mary, Mother of God no! Oh no, Mammy help!"

The others turned back on hearing Seosamh's screams. Eric put his hand on Damien's shoulder.

"Damien, stay here with the sword, I'll get your brother!"

Giving Damien the sword, Eric darted back to help Seosamh. Damien was astonished because not only did the sword feel so heavy in his hands but he saw Eric grab onto the oncoming slab and slowly, painfully managing to push it back up with his raw strength. All of his energy went into stopping the slab. Fortunately for Eric, the very sight of him gave Seosamh the strength and determination to pull himself up and limp towards the entrance.

The other two grabbed onto Seosamh, dragging him aside just as the slab slammed against the floor, permanently sealing the chamber off from the rest of the world. That didn't matter to them since they now had the sword. Eric took the sword in his hands again while Damien embraced Seosamh. For now, the three sat there panting. Looking at his watch, Eric asked the boys. "Boys, do you realise it is six o'clock in the morning?"

Seosamh protested, "What? But we went in at midnight, how could it be..."

"Ah, I should have warned you that the Tuatha De Dánann, the people who built that place were faeries or what your people called the "Aós Sidhé". Time operates differently in their realm."

Seosamh slumped back down onto the ground as he groaned in despair.

"OH NO!! We're later than we hoped, I hope Mammy and Daddy are still asleep...otherwise I cannot bear to think of all the chores we'll have to do as punishment...come on Damien, let's go home."

Seosamh tried to stand up only to collapse back down with immense pain in his ankle.

Frustrated, he then said. "Sweet Lord, I think I've broken it..."

Eric studied the boy's ankle.

"Your parent's anger is going to be the least of your worries because I think that boy needs some medical attention."

It was clear that they were almost at the foot of the staircase because they could now hear the crows outside croaking. Eric turned to Damien.

"Come on, help him up, I'll give you a ride home and explain everything to your parents. They should be proud that you two found something that entire armies and empires have failed to find, chop! chop!"

Slowly, the three started up the stairs. Even louder than the crows was the sound of Oisín barking.

3

A Sword of light

Eric was baffled to see Oisín come running down the steps.

"Hold on boy, we're coming up...slow down, what's the matter with you?"

Oisín then ran up the stairs and then back down again. Eric paused.

"Behind me if you please, if Oisín's barking like that it means that there is something wrong."

The first thought of Seosamh and Damien was that their parents not only knew of their absence from home but had also sent the guards to look for them. Neither of them were looking forward to reuniting with their parents. They reached the top of the stairs and stepped out in the open air again. Looking around him, Damien could see that it was bright but cloudy outside and he could once again see plenty of crows. Ahead of him, Eric stopped and his eyes widened. The boys looked around in dread.

"Oh no, are these the guards?" Seosamh stuttered.

"No, they wouldn't be armed if they were guards. Plus, they are not in uniform either."

Circling around Eric and the boys were men in dark long coats and flat caps. They wore Celtic crosses around their necks as opposed to the simple cross worn around Eric's neck. Their leaders wore Fedoras and they were armed with a variety of firearms including revolvers, semi-automatic pistols, and rifles.

One man even had a Thompson gun clasped in his gloved hands. Alarmed and confused, Eric reached for his own Luger pistol which was in his pocket but the leader pointed his own

Mauser pistol at him.

"Don't even think about it! Mr. Trent!"

Eric was alarmed.

"Well, who are you? How do you know my name? Come on, speak up! What do you want from me?"

The leader of the team retorted harshly.

"You have done this country a great violation, Mr. Eric Trent! You, a man of Norman blood have dared to lay his hands upon one of her greatest treasures! On behalf of our beloved Ireland, we demand "An Claíomh Solais"!"

Eric sighed, asking,

"Oh, for the love of God, you're the IRA, are you not? Why would folk like you have those weapons, unless you are working with the Nazis?? Listen sir! I am not an English spy, I'm merely an archaeologist!"

"IRA! Is that what you think we are? We have no time for the IRA or the Nazis! If that Teutonic Sadist from the continent comes near our Island, then we will bleed his armies till they are as white as a corpse!"

"Well, if you are not a bunch of republicans, blue shirts or unionists, then who are you?"

"We are the "Druids". We serve on behalf of Lord Donacagh, high king of the Society of Saint Patrick! We seek "An Claíomh Solais". Give it over now."

Eric felt even more shocked and surprised.

"The sword? You mean the one I'm holding now? How did you know what I was doing here? I've never met any of you before..."

Two of the druids made way as a voice that Eric knew spoke.

"It was the best thing to do, Mr. Trent."

Both Seosamh and Damien gasped. Eric's fear and surprise transformed into hatred and disgust as he saw Calum coming up beside the Druids.

"Calum McKeone, well if it is not my overseer? My trusted friend who offered to help me find resources when no other took me seriously."

Calum gathered his courage because looking at Eric's face was not an easy thing to do. He replied staunchly.

"They offered me three thousand pounds! This sword does not belong in a museum, not even an Irish one. Did you really think I would allow you to get away with your glorified thievery of our treasure!"

Eric's voice was full of contempt.

"I trusted you; you offered me support, I saw you as loyal! YOU TREACHEROUS SNAKE!!! You don't care about the artefact. You betrayed me for a bribe of THREE THOUSAND POUNDS!!!"

Both boys looked surprised as they saw Eric lunging towards Calum as if to bloody his face with his fists only for a Druid to fire off his gun.

The Druid leader snapped at Eric.

"Enough, Mr. Trent, what Calum did was noble. Make this easy for us and yourself and HAND OVER THE SWORD!"

Eric felt frustrated, he had just risked his life and Seosamh had broken his ankle for that sword. He was not going to give it up like that. He glared at the Druid leader.

"What happens if I don't comply?"

The boys felt a surge of dread while Oisín howled in despair.

"If ye don't comply, we'll kill the boys so that this village will know the cost of working with a Norman Protestant! Oh, and we'll shoot your dog as well."

"What?? Wait a minute, that's not fair, they are only boys from an Irish speaking village at that! No, if you are shooting anyone, you are shooting me. I'm the outlander you wish to see gone, fine! THEN SHOOT ME!! IT WAS MY IDEA TO COME HERE AND DIG UP THE SWORD IN THE NAME OF ARCHAEOLOGY!!!"

"No, you must live and they must die so that you may see the pain that you have brought when ye go thieving.... now give us the sword and we'll all go unharmed!!"

Eric now realized he was facing a difficult choice. The fact that this group would kill children to further their goals fuelled his heart with rage. He looked back at the boys and saw them embracing each other with their eyes closed. The druids raised their guns at them.

"On the count of three, Trent!! One!! Two! Thr..."

Eric raised his hand.

"Stop! Take this. Take this sword if you must!"

The Druids lowered their guns and Eric approached their leader. He presented the sword to them. Oisín growled at Calum who was eager to receive his money as reward.

Suddenly the sun began to shine upon the blade. The crows rose in a black cloud to fly away from the area. Oisín started to bark loudly. Both Damien and Seosamh opened their eyes as they felt an ominous presence. Something was about to happen.

The men of the Society of Saint Patrick turned and began to flee to their cars and motorbikes. Calum shouted after them.

"Wait, wait a second, what about my money?"

"You'd better run, Calum!"

Calum looked back nervously as the wind blew against his face. Curious at this unexpected turn of events, Eric looked at the sword and found that as the sun's rays shone down on the sword, the symbols lit up in a glowing yellow colour. Damien was shouting at him.

"Boss? Boss what in the name of God is going on?"

As he raised the sword up, Eric was filled with increasing anxiety.

"It's glowing...it's glowing! Of course, it is the Sword of Light, it's.... EVERYONE, DUCK AND GET DOWN!! DON'T LOOK!!"

Without even thinking, Damien and Seosamh ducked down while

Calum looked on in awe.

Eric yelled at him.

"You fool! Get down! Don't look!"

"As if you know anything about the artefact, Trent…"

Eric was speechless as the sword glowed brighter and brighter until it let out an explosive burst of light. Eric felt dazed and stumbled but the blast scorched the nearby trees, shaving them bare. It also enveloped Calum in fire. He screamed loudly and ran towards the cliff. He was in sheer agony as he felt that his skin was starting to melt off his bones. Calum ran straight off the cliff and plummeted screaming into the icy waters of the sea, and deep below the depths. Eric covered his eyes to shield them from the blinding light of the sword. Once the blast had gone, the smoking hot sword tumbled to the ground. Eric slumped down and only roused when he felt Oisín licking his face.

"Hello, Oisín, I'm glad you are always there."

Eric patted Oisín on the head as he stood up.

Seosamh and Damien helped each other up and gazed at the burnt trees. The Druids were now gone and Calum was nowhere to be seen. Horrified by the sight, Seosamh finally found his voice.

"What in the name of the Virgin Mary was that? Did that come from the sword?"

"I don't know, let's pray that the sword doesn't end up in the North. One can only imagine what the B-specials would do with it if they got their hands on it!"

The boys went over to Eric as he picked up the sword, looking at it in horror. He went over to his car and opened the boot. Fearful of his expression, they waited for him to speak.

"This artefact must become the property of the National History Museum. It must not be marketed as a weapon for it can melt skin like candle wax."

"Do you even know how that happened? Did the sword do that?" Damien faltered.

"Yes, the sword did that. How it happened, I don't know, probably something to do with the effect of the sun.... but.... I know far too many countries that would conquer all of Ireland to find out."

Upon hearing that, both boys looked at each other with dread. Eric then clapped his hands. "Come on you two, let's get both of you home."

Willingly, the boys followed Eric to the car.

If there was one good thing that the boys got out of this venture, it was that they got a ride home in Eric's car, which was far more advanced than any other the boys had seen. Damien was sitting beside Eric while Seosamh was sitting in the back seat beside Oisín. The sword was tucked firmly in the boot of the car so that no one could disturb it. Seosamh was excited because he had never been in a car. He gazed wide-eyed at countryside around him. Eric had his eyes on the road while the music of Charles Trenet played on his radio. Damien was curious about the amount of French items in Eric's car.

"Mr. Trent? Sir? May I ask you something?"

Switching off the radio, Eric nodded.

"Mr. Trent, for an Englishman, you sure have a taste for French things. I mean, bottles of champagne, music of Charles Trenet, a Parisian singer and even a book of Balzac. Why's that?"

"It's because I grew up in Paris, my parents took me there when I was just an infant. As a result, I developed French tastes. Then the war came and the Germans took France, so I came to London and worked as an archaeologist."

In the backseat, Seosamh examined the door beside his seat and pressed a button on it. The window came down, letting in a burst of wind that lapped against his face. Surprised, he switched the button again to cause the window to go back up. Eventually the car reached the village. But little did they know, the crows were following them.

When they arrived at the town, the children that were out in the streets got excited as they saw the car pull in. Having never seen such a vehicle like this, they ran over to it. The children crowded around the car, forcing Eric to drive as slowly as possible through the streets of the town. Eric also sounded the car horn, causing it to make a honking noise in an attempt to get the children out of the way of the vehicle. Many of the older villagers also came towards the car to see it, for they had not seen a vehicle like this before.

"What's going on, am I the town hero or what?" Eric asked at last.

"No sir, they've just never seen a car since the beginning of the Emergency. Especially a car that looks like this."

"I see, but all the same, some people in this country still have motor vehicles."

Donal and Sarah were together when they heard all the noise outside. Hurrying out, Sarah muttered under her breath.

"If that's them, I'll kill the pair of them for running off like that..."

But as the car came to a halt outside their house, she faltered as Eric stepped out of the car. Eric tipped his hat with his gloved hand.

"Mrs O'Laoghaire, I presume?"

"Eh....yes, are ye his boss sir?"

"Yes, I'm Trent, Eric Trent."

Sarah was speechless because Eric was not what she was expecting when she heard that he was Damien's "English boss". Eric was a handsome, imposing man. Momentarily, she couldn't help but be captivated by him. She snapped out of this though.

"Mr. Trent, do you know where my son Damien is, he's sixteen years of age and he works for ye. He and his younger brother

Seosamh have gone missing and…"

"Don't worry, Madam, the boys are safe with me. I found them at the dig site."

"What? The dig site?? Oh sir, you don't realize just how worried I was, they left without me knowing what they were doing…"

"Don't worry, personally I think you should be proud of your sons. They helped me find "An Claíomh Solais" and in turn they have won three hundred pounds as a reward for their troubles."

"An Claíomh Solais"? You mean you found one of the four mythical treasures of Ireland. But what about Seosamh, is he alright?"

Seeing Damien help Seosamh emerge from the car, Sarah asked.

"Mr. Trent? What happened to Seosamh?"

"Em…yes….Madame, I do hope you are good at the art of medicine because I can't find a hospital in miles."

"But why is Seosamh limping?"

"Madame, please, come inside, I can explain everything."

Sarah cautiously followed Eric inside the house as he passed by Donal. Donal could only look on with hostility. Damien and Seosamh came up to the door. Although he was glad to have them back, Donal spoke to Damien.

"So, is this the English boss you've been working for?"

"Yes, father, but don't worry, he's a good man."

The crows were still observing them as they entered the house.

The afternoon in the O'Laoghaires house was surprisingly more pleasant than what Eric expected. Seosamh had his ankle bandaged up, Eric was treated as an honoured guest and the twins took a liking to his dog. The creature was after all, a gentle giant.

***

But in the evening, after dinner, Donal and Eric settled in the armchairs on either side of the fireplace. The children had gone to bed and the room was quiet as Donal lit his pipe. As Finally Donal spoke.

"So, I presume you've come for more than just hospitality, have you Eric?"

"Alas, you've got that right, yes, for I will need some assistance in bringing the sword to Dublin. It is on one hand, a very precious artefact but on the other hand, it is one of the most dangerous objects that I have ever touched. It can melt someone's face. It melted my overseer, dooming him to a dreadful and most agonizing death. His corpse lies in the deep after he fell off a cliff."

"Well, you should count yourself lucky that the corpse is gone because I assure you the guards aren't so superstitious and they would charge you for murder. Anyway, what do you want from us?"

"Mr. O'Laoghaire, as you are the man of this house, I ask you for permission to take Damien with me to Dublin to work as my assistant."

Donal's eyes widened in shock.

"What? You wish to take my son to Dublin? A city built by Norsemen and rife with slums. Dublin is a sorry place, Mr. Trent....what makes you think that I would consent to that?"

"Mr. O'Laoghaire, if you please, Dublin is not the city it was in 1916. The Irish National History Museum is a most marvellous place to explore, it will be the eventual resting place of the sword and your son deserves to go there. Without him, I'd still be digging out there tomorrow just like every other day I've been in this country."

Donal considered for a few moments.

"Did you talk to Damien about this? I would like to hear his voice on the matter before any decision is made. Mark me, Mr. Trent, I don't want to see him made a slave and tricked with false promises."

"My promise is not false and I have no intention of making him a slave. Once the presentation is done and the sword is in its rightful place, I will bring Damien right back home to you. How about we sleep on it?"

Donal sighed and nodded his consent.

4

Damien's Journey Begins

Little did Eric or the O'Laoghaires know, but outside in the dark of the night, in the dimly lit town, a crow was perched on one of the electric poles observing the house. After some time, the creature took off and flew into the night, away from the town and towards an ancient mound from before the time of the Celts. As it entered the mound, the crow passed through some form of mist and soon into what looked like a world of twisted brambles and claw like trees. Within this underworld, shadowy figures observed the crow as it perched itself on one of the gnarled branches. A large shadowy figure approached and spoke in a deep voice.

"Well, crow, what news do you bring about the world above?"

Suddenly the crow responded.

"I bring news of "An Claíomh Solais", my Lord Brés of the Fomorians. It has been found by mortal humans!!"

"What? Humans?"

The mention of this caused all the different creatures to howl and growl. Lord Brés roared his anger.

"Humans? When the tribe of Milesian Celts invaded, the Tribe of Danu buried that sword in a complex so deep that not even a Fomorian could find it! How did a species so primitive and pathetic find it?"

The crow recounted his story.

"The human boys were led by a stranger from the land of Albion, a country known as Britain since Brutus of Troy conquered its giants all those years ago. The same country that Arthur came from. Though they spoke of him as an Englishman, he looked strangely familiar, my Lord. He was much stronger than a normal human yet he dressed like one."

"Familiar, yes? What colour was his hair? This man of Albion?"

"As red as fire, his skin was as pale as marble and his eyes as blue as saltwater!"

Brés grunted.

"I see, that sounds awfully like Lugh. Follow him and see where he takes the sword. Inform all the creatures of the night, let them be our army."

Another creature voiced a question.

"My Lord, do we have any idea of where he is going?"

The crow preened himself before answering.

"I believe he is headed to the place they call "Dublin", a city built by Norsemen....but I warn you, the world of men has changed considerably since we lost against them last. That was in the time of King Arthur."

The following morning, in the sitting room, Damien was packing his suitcase with what little he had. Aidan and Eileen watched him solemnly.

"So, Damien, you're packing up your stuff. Are ye leaving us?"

"Don't worry, I'm just going to Dublin. Hopefully, if all things go well, I should be back when it's done."

"What are ye doing?"

"I'm taking a magic sword to the museum, so it can be preserved in safe hands."

"When will ye be back?"

Damien sighed.

"I....I don't know."

All of the children, including Seosamh, who was sitting on one of the chairs with a bandaged foot looked up at Damien with saddened eyes. Eileen threw her arms around Damien saying. "We're going to miss ye, Damien."

Damien reached down to give her a cuddle.

"I know, I'll miss ye too."

He went into the hall. Donal was waiting for him at the door.

"So, Damien? You've accepted his proposal, have ye? You're leaving us to go to Dublin?"

"Yes, I have made my choice...I must, I need to see the museum. I can't stay here."

Donal nodded slowly.

"Damien, your mother and I should've known that you would leave this place someday. That was no surprise since there's not enough in this town to do for a young man such as yourself. That's what all your mates did, they left this place and never came back. Damien, this town is dying."

Damien put his hand on his father's shoulder.

"Dad, I will never forget this place, or anything you've done for me. But think of it, this town, thought to be worthless, was the resting place of "An Claíomh Solais". Surely that will put us on the map and maybe something will be done about the poverty here."

"Mark me, Damien, don't be afraid to think for yourself, it will help you survive in that city."

Damien and Donal embraced. Damien turned to his mother who blessed him with holy water, then hugged him.

"Ye'll be alright in Dublin, won't you Damien?"

"Eh....of course, Mam, don't worry, the War hasn't reached us yet so I'll be fine."

"God bless ye, Damien."

Outside, Eric was waiting by the car looking solemnly at the house. Oisín slumped down beside him, his ears drooping. Eric patted him on the head.

"You'll miss the children, won't you, Oisín?"

Eric went back to say goodbye to Donal and Sarah.

"I hope you can trust me; he should be back when this whole affair with the sword is done. I'm sorry if I have left you both miserable."

However, Donal merely put his out his hand to Eric.

"Mark me, Sassenach, it was inevitable that Damien was going to leave this place the moment he left the cradle. He is his own man, what matters is that he trusts ye."

Eric tipped his fedora to the O'Laoghaires.

"Thank you both, for your hospitality. I'd still be digging here if it weren't for your son."

And with that Eric went back to his car. Damien got into the front alongside Eric while Oisín crawled onto the backseat. As Eric started the engine of the car, Damien waved one last time to his family as they all waved farewell before closing the door.

As the car hit the road, it kicked up clouds of dust. Damien felt a heavy weight on his heart as he saw his town grow smaller and smaller. He was painfully aware that he would not be seeing his hometown for some time, and that meant everything he knew. Eric observed him from the corner of his eye.

"You're going to miss your home, are you?"

"Don't ye?"

"Oh...yes, I do, Paris was a most marvellous place, it wasn't easy to see the Wehrmacht triumphantly march under the Arc de Triomphe. That's not even getting into the home I never knew."

Damien raised his eyebrows.

"You're not really even English, are ye, sir?"

Eric starred fixedly at the road ahead.

"I'll tell you a secret. My parents were from a lost land known as Agartha. We were a fair skinned people with blonde or red hair and we used magic to build our society."

"You mean like the "Tuatha De Danann"?"

"Yes, I believe we were the same species. We called ourselves Tileans, we were native to the land of Thule, a land that doesn't exist anymore. It was lost in the Great Deluge."

"What happened to your people, Mr. Trent?"

Eric sighed sadly.

"We were mostly wiped out by an invading horde of monsters. My parents survived but I was born after the purge. We were conquered and dispersed, not too differently from your people."

"Why do you sound English then if you are not an Englishman at all?"

"Because I inherited the accent from my father. He was born to a Tilean woman and a British archaeologist. He was a good man and well mannered."

Eric's words made Damien think very differently about Eric all of a sudden. All the unnatural aspects of Eric suddenly made sense. It was strange to discover that this Oxford sounding man had more in common to the Tribe of Danu than the Irish themselves. The car headed for Castlebar, the main town in County Mayo.

When they reached Castlebar, Eric and Damien went immediately to the station. Damien was already getting quite a shock because the station was bustling with activity as flocks of passengers headed for the platform. Railway guards checked the tickets of passengers. Several of these guards held red or green flags that would be used to signal the train. Eric bought two first class tickets from the counter while Damien gazed around him. As they headed for a carriage, curiosity got the better of him.

"Mr. Trent? Have you told others of your secret?"

"Not many know of my true lineage, Damien, consider yourself lucky. I wouldn't even trust politicians with that secret."

Eventually, the two settled into their seats on the train and Eric kept the "Claíomh Solais" firmly shut in a suitcase, safe from the sun's rays. There was a warning note attached to the suitcase.

"Do not open when the sun is shining or under a full moon at all costs."

Eric put the suitcase above their seat. Damien saw the other first-class passengers look at him with odd expressions. Damien wondered what it was about him which made him conspicuous. He watched Eric take out a book entitled "Le Colonel Chabert".

"Mr. Trent, are you sure you should be reading that?"

"Why not?"

Eric lowered his book.

"Who in the name of God would censor "Le Colonel Chabert"; it's a very chaste book about a cavalry officer regaining his honour!"

"Eh....the Church?"

"Don't say the church, this book is French, the Catholic Church was French as well. Don't worry young man, there's nothing obscene about this book. Then again, anything can be made obscene by a sensitive idiot in a position of power."

"I'm not saying there was anything obscene in your book, sir."

"Well, that's good."

At that moment, the whistle of the Locomotive squealed as smoke began to emit from its funnel. Railway guards rang their bells while telling passengers to get aboard. The train soon began its loud and smoky journey out of the station and moved smoothly along the rails. Hearing the noise of the engine was enough to tell Damien that he was now past the point of no return.

That evening, as the train made its way across Ireland, the

two had dinner on the train. It was a dinner in which Damien got a taste of fine foods and even got a taste of Jameson.

"Even during an "Emergency", you aristocrats still dine in style. Right?"

Eric laughed.

"Of course, we do, we drank our wine through the Black Death, we drank our wine through the Revolution, we dined in style when the Titanic was struck and even during the Great Depression. We wouldn't be aristocrats if we didn't do what we did with some sense of style."

Damien couldn't help but laugh.

"Mr. Trent, you should have brought Seosamh on this journey. He may have been born poor but he is an aristocrat at heart and wants to go to America. Trust me, when he grows up, he wants to be like Clark Gable or Errol Flynn…"

"I'm afraid there was no way I could bring him with me on this endeavour. His ankle was broken in his efforts to help retrieve the sword and he is only a boy of twelve. I seriously doubt your mother would have consented."

Eric refilled his glass when suddenly Oisín barked and jumped up and put his front paws on the table, taking everyone nearby by surprise. Eric was angry.

"Oisín! Get down! Get down from there you old renegade!"

But the dog kept barking at the window.

"Oisín, get down! Now!"

The dog retreated to the floor leaving the other passengers baffled. Eric looked embarrassed. "Pardon us, our dog is a little jumpy."

But Damien had another idea.

"Boss, are you sure he wasn't trying to tell us something? You said that he wouldn't bark unless it was important, didn't ye?"

"Oh…well, yes, but what on earth could it be?"

Eric trailed off when he saw that outside in the darkening

sky, a crow was flying by the train carriage. The bird even looked as if it was staring straight at Eric. He was baffled. Never had he experienced anything like this before.

"Damien, is it natural for a crow to be following us everywhere? I swear that crow has been following us…"

"Crows? Like at the dig site? They were everywhere when we showed up there, Mr. Trent."

"Indeed, well there is one following us right now, I swear it. It's as if it is spying on us. Is that natural?"

"Not for a normal crow, perhaps it's the Morrigan, boss?"

"Who?"

"The Morrigan, Mr. Trent, she was a goddess associated with birth and death. Her name means "Phantom Queen"".

Eric sat back down.

"Phantom Queen? Oh, good God, there's no country in the English-speaking world more mystically bizarre than Ireland. It shamelessly mashes Christian morality and scientific logic with pagan superstitions. What other place in Western Europe has people fearing wailing ghost women while listening to the radio and taking the motor car to work at the same time?"

Damien didn't know how to respond to that. For that was a common observation for foreigners to make of Ireland as a country. By the time he looked back at Eric, Eric was dozing off to sleep. Oisín was now sleeping under the table. What Damien did not know was that Eric was once again having his dreams.

This time, Eric was having the dream about the battle again where he was leading the army of towering fair skinned warriors against what looked to be horned monsters with long white hair and icy eyes. In the dream, he was a very different person, he was in armour, he had thick red hair and a beard, and he clasped a powerful lance, larger than any lance he had seen before. His body was patterned with tattoos and he plunged the lance into a monster, killing it easily. The warriors all wielded swords similar to the one he and Damien had just dug up; they used these weapons to melt through the monsters. The druids of both armies exchanged explosive bursts of magic at each other and at the enemy army. However, in the distance, he heard a roar and he readied a sling. Looking up, he could see a horned giant that towered above the coast.

It was as this creature roared that Eric suddenly woke up from his dream. The dreams themselves left Eric confused. Why was he having these dreams ever since he came to Ireland, what were they trying to tell him? Dreams like this guided him to the sword. He read more of "Le Colonel Chabert" in an attempt to get his mind off the whole nightmare.

A few hours later the train finally arrived in Dublin city, screeching to a halt in Houston station. Being a young boy from a remote country town left Damien to be taken by surprise at the sheer numbers of people he saw walk past him as he and Eric left the station. Eric held Oisín firmly by the leash as he set his foot on the cobblestone pavement of Dublin city. As he navigated Dublin, Damien could see plenty of barges, steamboats and even sailing boats going up and down the Liffey. People skidded across the pavements on their bicycles while trams packed with passengers went up and down, powered by electric lines that criss-crossed the city.

Newsboys screamed out the latest headlines as they held out the newspapers to be sold while uniformed guards observed the streets. Though unarmed, they were well trained earning them a healthy respect from the crowds that they watched. This meant that their presence was enough to deter any brawling. Damien even saw soldiers dressed in khaki uniforms and with rifles slung over their shoulders pass by him. Eric studied the crowds around him.

"Isn't it ironic, Damien?"

"What's ironic, boss?"

"Only 24 years ago, this city would have been torn up by gunfire and bombardments while the rest of Europe was dancing and drinking. Now, it is totally in reverse."

"In what way?"

"Life goes on here as if nothing ever happened while Britain is being bombarded by these devices known as V-1 rockets...many in England envy you."

"Ah yes, that's what it looks like...but everything is rationed here. Businesses have shut down; many lads are without work. That's why you had such a willing workforce when you came to go digging."

"I see..."

Damien felt as if he had walked into another country as he walked the streets of Dublin.

As the two walked up Grafton Street, they approached Saint Stephen's Green. Every so often large double decker buses coloured in green stopped by the Park to drop off passengers. These people looked more glamorously dressed and more formal than anyone Damien had met or seen before.

"So where is the Museum, Mr. Trent?"

"Eh, not too far from where we are, although we might take a tram to get us there."

Damien was very excited.

"Well let's go then!"

But Eric didn't move.

"Oh no, not just yet."

"What, why?"

Eric's eyes were stern as he looked at Damien.

"You, sir, are not going to mix with Ireland's top brass dressed like a village boy from the Connemara. I'm going to be blunt with you, Damien, we can't bring the sword to the museum with you looking like this. They'll laugh at you and won't take you seriously."

Damien's face fell.

"They'll laugh at me? These are my best clothes that Ma washed and ironed for this occasion. Besides, I thought these people were Irish."

Eric felt bad for Damien but he continued firmly.

"Oh, my dear boy, I am so dreadfully sorry but class snobbery is as old as civilization itself. Even the Marxists for all their talk of classless society have little time for common people dressed in "common garb". The thing about ruling classes is that they care little for your genius or inner nobility, they care about the way you look. Trust me, Damien, my grandmother learnt this the hard way."

Damien felt hurt when he heard this, especially because he was aware that Eric was probably right. Eric had more experience with high society than he did, having grown up in Paris. On the other hand, he desperately wanted to see the museum for himself.

"And what do you propose, Mr. Trent?"

"Well come with me, Damien. You need a bath, a proper shave, and a suit. I would also advise you to read some of Jane Austen's books. No one wrote more brilliantly about society manners than she did."

That afternoon, Eric rented an apartment in the Georgian area of Dublin. This place was notably more peaceful and calmer than the rest of the city and had a large array of ornate houses that looked almost like little mansions. Such houses were built back in the 18th century by the Anglo-Norman aristocracy that ruled Ireland back then. It was in this apartment that Damien was now reading "Pride and Prejudice" while he luxuriated in a long bath.

He was fascinated to discover that the England he had been raised to hate was painted in a completely different light. Suddenly, England and its people felt strangely more human and less distant as he continued to read. Later on, Damien had a trip to the barber so that his oak brown hair was now neat and tidy.

After that, Eric took him to the tailor shop to get a suit. Damien felt awkward as the tailor took his measurements. Eric tried to encourage him.

"Look on the bright side, Damien, when you go home to your village, all the girls will be swooning over you with such a fine suit. Soon, they might even want you to marry them."

"I can't go back to Mayo in a suit, I'll get it mucky…besides I'm only sixteen."

"Damien, with a three hundred pounds reward, you should be able to get yourself an adequate job, a secure income and perhaps even education. There are marvellous colleges in this country."

"What about my town?"

"Surely with that bright mind of yours, you could even find a way to attract investment to your town. By coming here with the sword you'll put your home on the map."

The tailor, having finished measuring Damien, led him away to try on a variety of suits.

By the time he came out of the shop, Damien wore a smart, dark grey suit. On his feet were shiny black laced shoes and a red tie was knotted around his neck. Eric had even added a cane and Fedora in an attempt to help Damien fit in. Damien had strange feelings when he dressed like this. On one hand, he received very different reactions, for now with the suit and his youthful tidy appearance, many of the girls his age could not take their eyes off him. Their smiles actually helped to lift his heart and make him feel less awkward or out of place.

On the other hand, he felt tight in this suit and he found he walked more slowly and less surely. Eric noticed this.

"Damien, straighten yourself. Stand tall and strong. You must start acting like a gentleman if you are to go near the museum."

Damien tried walking like that but rather than feeling a sense of confidence, he felt even more awkward, like he was being something completely alien to his own nature. Seeing this, Eric patted Damien on the shoulder.

"Listen, don't worry, as soon as this is done you can change back into your original clothes. I understand it can be difficult to be a stranger to the top brass of society."

"How would you know? You were born into this class. You understand their mannerisms."

"Trust me, Damien, I've been an outsider since I was born, even in Paris and London."

5

Disrupted Presentation

Night settled over Dublin. The city was lit up by electric streetlamps which illuminated the area. A week had passed since their arrival in Dublin and at last everything was ready for the presentation of the sword to the museum. In the apartment, Damien looked into the mirror and saw the reflection of a smartly dressed young man. He could hardly believe what he was seeing because for so many years this was the type of moment he had been waiting for. A moment in which he was on his way up the social ladder. He looked cleaner now and no longer was his body roughened and hardened by dirt and bitter hard labour. As he posed, he thought of how so many of his kinsmen had to cross the stormy Atlantic, leaving everything behind as they sought wealth and prosperity in America. He, on the other hand, had the chance to achieve such success in Ireland.

He should have been happy: he was not in his town anymore, he now had modern conveniences such as baths, electric heating and electric lights, he even had a room to himself. He was now speaking English far more than he ever had, he was even reading English novels like "Pride and Prejudice", "Phineas Finn" or "The Time Machine". The one thing he wasn't reading was the unique myths that built up the lore of his country. It made him wonder if he was giving up too much for material comfort. Such things were concepts he had never thought much about before and he had even bemoaned his father for thinking about them. Suddenly, Damien heard barking by the door. Oisín came bounding across the room to him, sitting down beside him. A wolfhound in a Georgian era building wasn't a common sight and it warmed Damien's heart. He gave Oisín a hug saying. "Hello, Oisín, you're coming as well, are ye?"

He stroked the dog, thinking that he was like Damien, a Celt, and he helped Damien cope with any home sickness that he had. Eric followed Oisín into the room.

"You really do like Oisín, don't you?"

Damien looked up to see Eric, dressed in a white suit with a red rose in his lapel, reach down to pat the dog on the head. Eric continued.

"I was but a boy of four when I first had that dog. Oisín was a pup who had been taken from his mother illegally to be sold on the black market. At the time, I was alone with few friends and my father discovered the puppy abandoned on the roadside. Feeling pity for such a gorgeous creature, my father took him back to our place. Gave him as a present to me for my birthday. Father had an interest in the Irish myths so he called him Oisín…"

Eric then said in a saddened tone, "He was the one friend I truly had. He grows old while I stay young and handsome. So many men crave longevity and those who have it long to renounce it."

Damien wasn't sure what to make of this.

"Oisín is coming with us, isn't he, boss?"

"Of course, he's coming, I'm not leaving him here on his own. Come on, Damien, chop, chop!"

Eric slipped on Oisín's leash and picking up the case with the sword, they went into the streets of Dublin. Damien found that the electric streetlights of the city made the experience of walking through the night much more comforting than it was before. Looking up, he could see the light of the moon partly coming through the clouds.

Arriving at the National Museum, Damien looked up in awe. The building looked like a palace with its front patterned by ornate pillars and statues. As it was nighttime, the building was brightly lit up. Several cars and carriages were parked outside the Museum entrance as glamorously dressed guests gathered outside.

Guards checked their invitations before letting them in. As he and Eric entered through the door, Damien looked up at the ceiling and saw mosaics of the different signs of the zodiac patterned in a circle. Curious, he pointed to them.

"Eric, do ye see that?"

"The signs of the Zodiac, yes, occultists believe that we pass through a solar year, symbolised by a sign of the Zodiac. We are currently in "Pisces": The year of the fish. We are also born under the different signs of the Zodiac. It is said that we are given unique characteristics based on the sign we are born under."

Damien found it difficult to speak because he had never seen architecture like this before except maybe in movies. The two entered the much larger main hall which was a huge room. The main hall had pillars all around it in a square like shape and at the centre of the hall was a vast array of artefacts in glass containers. The room was populated by guests in elegant outfits that were observing the artefacts while drinks were being distributed by waiters. The sight of waiters with wine and the sound of orchestral music playing in the background made Damien think for a while that he was in London, not Dublin. Everyone around him spoke English in refined voices and the whole scene made him think of films that he once saw in the cinema house in his town when it was still open.

Damien felt both excited and nervous as he walked across the smooth floor surrounded by the various guests. He tried to smile politely but they were all looking at him. Some of the guests muttered to each other as they saw Oisín.

"Is that a wolf hound, Good Lord this gentleman, Mr. Trent, has unusual taste, bringing such an ugly creature into hallowed halls. Don't you think George?"

"Yes, indeed, my dear Elisabeth, an ugly creature indeed, so terribly out of place on this occasion. But then again, he was born on a burning Zeppelin according to tales I heard, and he grew up among the French, that explains why his tastes are so terribly distorted."

"A burning Zeppelin? How was that possible, how could any woman manage that?"

Damien's attempted smile turned to a smirk of contempt towards the two, he wasn't too keen on hearing them talk about Oisín like that.

"Mr. Trent? What sort of people are these folk?"

"Self-proclaimed archaeologists, historians maybe, aristocrats who wouldn't risk their ankle for a higher cause. Don't mind them Damien, Oisín and I are well used to poorly delivered insults, like bullets bouncing off a tank..."

Then Eric heard a voice he recognised asking,

"Well, well, if it is not the son of Keith and Elinor Trent? Eric, you look well dressed for the occasion!"

Amazed and overjoyed, Eric turned to see an elderly man with a waxed moustache. Seeing him, Eric asked.

"Mr. Harker? Mr. Quincy Harker, head of the Pellucidar Expeditionary Corps....so good to see you!!"

Quincy and Eric shook hands.

"The pleasure is mine, Eric, congratulations on your find!"

Eric turned to Damien and said.

"Damien, this is Quincy Harker, he was my father's boss. Mr. Harker, this is Damien O'Laoghaire, a young Irishman from County Mayo who helped me dig up "An Claíomh Solais", and the main reason I was able to bring the artefact to the museum."

Turning to Damien, Quincy said,

"Ah....splendid, you already look like a gentleman, Mr O'Laoghaire. How do you feel about yourself?"

Damien was unsure on how to respond to that. He muttered.

"Eh...good...I guess..."

Damien's cheeks went as red as tomatoes due to embarrassment. Quincy chuckled.

"Ah, I see, the Irish don't have time for long winded speeches, always so blunt about things."

"Is that a bad trait sir?"

"On the contrary, I find the bluntness of the Irish Celts honest, and that honesty appeals to me. In England, villains mask their malice through refined manners and "false graces"."

"Quincy, why have you actually come here?" asked Eric.

"I've come to see your sword of course, see it up close before it is contained in a glass box. Follow me, Eric."

Curious and weary, Eric followed Quincy to a nearby bench that was next a pillar while Damien was left with Oisín.

"Eric, could you show me the sword?" Quincy's voice was urgent. Eric placed the suitcase on the bench and opened it. Quincy gazed in awe at the sword. Not only was it large for even a broadsword but despite being silver, it was now glowing in a golden colour. Seeing this, Quincy muttered under his breath.

"My God….the sword of light, the real sword of light."

He slowly took off his gloves and reached out a hand to the sword. Eric reached out a hand to stop him.

"Quincy? Quincy no!!"

As Quincy touched the blade, his fingers felt as if they just touched boiling water and recoiled. Quincy gasped as he now saw that his fingertips were red as if burnt. He turned back to Eric. "Has it always glowed like this?"

"Not when we first found it underground, but it has since absorbed the rays of the sun. There is a reason they call it the Sword of Light, Mr. Harker."

Quincy seemed bewitched by the glow of the sword.

"Magnificent, Eric, your father would be impressed. Now I have a proposal for you."

Eric raised his eyebrows.

"Quincy, you are a good friend, yes, but why are you really here?"

"As you have known since you were nine years of age, my organisation, the Pellucidar Expeditionary Corps has dealt with the paranormal and has fought supernatural monstrosities with the latest technology that is available."

"I know that, my father worked for you."

"Well ever since the war, we have served on behalf of Mr Churchill who receives my support when it comes to supernatural occurrences. He has taken interest in your dig."

Eric started to feel alarmed.

"I don't like where this is going but carry on."

"Eric, you know that this sword can channel the sun and send its rays into the enemy. Such a sword was a basic hand weapon of the Tuatha De Danann."

"Quincy, don't even think of that…"

"There will be three thousand pounds more to your treasury if you hand the sword over as a weapon to be used in "Operation Overlord", Adolf Hitler would be terrified!"

Eric was horrified. "No! No! No! JUST NO!"

Eric's face contorted with anguish as he continued.

"Listen sir! Even if I were to be gassed, I would never hand over this artefact. You don't even know what this thing truly is. I have seen this sword melt my overseer Calum McKeone like candle wax and the vegetation nearby was burnt to a crisp! I am not condemning conscripted beardless boys to such a grotesque demise! Is that understood?"

Quincy seemed unsurprised.

"So be it, Eric, I merely pass on the message from Mr. Churchill. I see you have inherited your father's old-fashioned sense of honour. Just know it will cost you any chance of the British government funding any more of your expeditions."

With that, Quincy walked off leaving Eric to stare. Although the two men were friends, there was no way he was handing the sword over for money. Little did he know but Damien had been listening to the conversation that he had with Quincy.

Having heard Eric's refusal, Damien thought more fondly of him as he was not driven by greed but by a genuine passion for seeking relics and preserving them. Beside him, Oisín growled. Without looking at him, Damien spoke his thoughts aloud.

"Oisín, you are blessed by God for ye have a good master."

Suddenly, Damien heard a voice from behind him.

"So, he's found the Claíomh Solais, has he?"

Turning around, Damien saw a towering, well-dressed man. His eyes were icy blue and he was clean-shaven. His raven hair was starting to become grey. Over his suit was a long coal black coat. Damien swallowed nervously.

"Who are ye? I'm Damien, Damien O'Laoghaire."

The man spoke harshly.

"I'm Lord Simon Fitzgerald, I now live in the North. I used to work for the Pellucidar Expeditionary Corps or P.E.C."

"Wait what? What's that? How do you know Eric?"

Simon took out a cigarette and lit it.

"I was part of an expedition that went to rescue Eric when he was a boy. It was in a place they called "Hollow Earth". P.E.C is an Anglo-American organisation but it firmly serves the British empire. It's headed by Quincy Harker."

"Quincy Harker? My Lord, I've just met Mr. Harker. Some friend he was, he tried to bribe Eric into giving the sword to him. To use as a weapon in the war!"

"Damn him, damn both of them. Damn Eric for digging up the sword and damn Quincy for wanting to use the sword as a weapon! Why? Do they not realise what that thing is? It's not just an ornament you can display in a museum or a country house! It is a..."

Eric interrupted the tirade.

"Yes, Lord Fitzgerald, it is a weapon and I know what it is capable of!"

Simon turned around and glared at Eric.

"Eric, if you know what it is capable of, then why in the name of God and his angels did you dig it up?"

"Listen, my Lord, the Irish National Museum is not motivated by Imperial interests. I just turned down an offer by Mr. Harker on behalf of the British government! An offer to use this sword to turn the tide of upcoming Operation Overlord!"

"Do you think he is the only one looking for that power?"

"Lord Fitzgerald, the Nazis won't come here, Ireland is neutral territory and there are too many German POWs to be used as a bargaining chip for them to risk an invasion. The Soviets are Marxists who don't believe in magic! The Japanese are too busy defending their islands to worry about this sword and Italy has been beaten utterly. Now if you'll excuse me, I have a presentation to make. My guests are waiting."

Eric and Damien walked off to prepare their presentation, leaving Simon to stare. Simon didn't follow and instead smoked another cigarette. Quincy Harker approached him.

"You are aware of the Fomorians, aren't you, Lord Fitzgerald?"

"Well, Mr. Harker, what interests you about the Fomorians?"

"They are a threat to the world, my Lord, defending the world with Western civilization's industrial might was my father's dream after he slew the Transylvanian count."

"Yet you serve the British government now, do you realize that Churchill might puppet your army and organisation to serve only the Empire's interests? He obviously sent you to find out about the sword."

Quincy sighed.

"I'm only siding with Churchill to defeat the Nazis, for their leader reeks of pure evil! But mark me Simon, I will not let the Empire control me and my men as if we are their slaves! Come, let us walk together."

Simon ground out his cigarette butt and followed Quincy through the corridors. Behind them, one of the drains moved as a clawed hand began to make its way out of the sewer.

Nobody, not even Eric, was aware that they were being watched or that something was happening as Damien helped Eric prepare the presentation. Damien and Eric handled the sword with the most delicate care as they placed it on the desk, near the door, Oisín's leash was attached to the wall. A crowd of guests gathered around to watch and listen. Eric composed himself and began.

"Ladies and Gentlemen, my name is Eric Trent and I would like to present "An Claíomh Solais", which means the "Sword of Light" in Gaelic."

As he said that, he pointed to the glowing sword.

"This sword was found in County Mayo with the help of my assistant here, Damien O'Laoghaire. As you see it is a broadsword in its design which is unusual for a sword in Celtic mythology, and it has the power to harness the sun's rays. If fully charged and fully harnessed, it can let out a blast of power more powerful than even a V2 rocket! That's if it is used properly of course."

The crowd rustled and muttered among themselves.

"Ladies and gentlemen, this country which we see as a "Celtic Periphery" may have once been the home to an ancient civilization more powerful than the Egyptians, the Hebrews of Solomon and maybe even the Romans…"

Suddenly, Eric was cut short by a haunting voice that echoed around the room.

"Ancient? We still exist, we wait in the shadows while you sleep. We are the darkness that you fear."

Eric's eyes widened in shock and anger while the crowd of guests became fearful. The room itself became much darker as the lights went off. This led the crowd to become even more anxious as they heard footsteps outside that were getting louder and louder. Damien was starting to feel his heart pound and Oisín began to growl angrily. Walking into the room and glowing in the darkness was a tall and imposing figure with an aquiline face. The creature had skin that was light grey and long silvery hair. His ears were like that of a bat while horns extended out of his forehead like a ram. His body was patterned with runes and tattoos and he had a curved sword sheathed to his belt. People within the crowd muttered to each other in fear and Eric looked completely shocked. The creature seemed strangely familiar as if he had seen it in his dreams but yet he had never really seen someone like this before.

Mustering his confidence, Eric forced himself to speak.

"Who are you? Why are you here?"

The creature glared at Eric with his icy eyes.

"I am King Brés, Lord of the Fomorians and Elven folk. I have come to claim what is mine!"

Eric's shock gave way to confusion.

"What? What do you mean? There is nothing here that belongs to you!"

Brés reached his pointy clawed hand towards Eric and spoke as if his patience was starting to wane.

"Give me the sword, Lugh! Give me the "Claíomh Solais"!"

Eric was shocked to hear himself being called "Lugh". Eric knew that Lugh was a half Fomorian and half Danann King who had led the Tuatha De Danann into battle against the Fomorian king Balor.

"Why do you call me Lugh? I'm Eric Trent, I'm from Agartha, but raised in France!"

"Just give me the sword! I have need of it!"

Eric's confusion turned to anger.

"Sword? The Claíomh Solais? What would a hideous apparition such as yourself want with the sword? What makes you think that you can just come in here and interrupt my presentation? Have you no sense of manners?"

"The manners of men mean little to me, Lugh."

"Do you really think you can take this artefact as a weapon of war? It belongs in a museum; you have no right to steal it!"

Brés smirked.

"Stealing? Is that not what humans do? Are all these artefacts not stolen? Is this land here not stolen? Stolen by their ancestors from the Tuatha De Danann. Isn't that what the Milesians did when they claimed Ireland as their own?"

Eric laughed harshly.

"You, sir, have no moral authority to condemn the humans. You are an unnatural invader from the otherworld! You tried to wipe out the Tuatha De Danann! You also made the tribe of Danu slaves and extorted them. You are no native of this dimension, let alone this country! You only bring destruction where mortal men build nations out of nothing! Don't even dare think I will hand this sword over to you!"

Brés reached his clawed hand and inflicted a painful scratch on Eric's cheek.

"Oh, I see, you are as stubborn as a brick wall, Lugh, unsurprising. Give me the sword or else…"

Eric forcefully slapped away Brés' hand.

"Or else what?"

"Or else, these guests of yours will all die!"

As Brés said this, hunched creatures with deformed bodies came out of the shadows. They had glowing yellowish eyes and large tusks similar to that of a Smilodon. Their skin was greenish grey and they had shaggy hair. In their clawed hands, they clasped spears and clubs. With this, the guests began to panic and some of them stood up to try to make their way out of there. Brés turned to them.

"Sit down!! Proud shallow creatures that you are!!!"

The people nervously sank back in their chairs, too terrified to move. Brés turned back to Eric.

"See these creatures, these are Fomorian grunts, goblins! Men also know them as Yahoos! Once given the order, they will not hesitate to indulge themselves in their sadistic pleasures. Give me the sword now or..."

Something stirred in Damien. He reached out his hand and grabbed the sword much to Brés' surprise.

Damien felt his body trembling but he gathered his courage and faced Brés.

"If you want to claim the sword, ye will have to take it from me!"

Damien pointed the Claíomh Solais at Brés. Furious at this defiance, he roared in terrifying tones.

"I SAID SIT DOWN! PEASANT!! Or I will unleash the grunts on your pitiful body!"

Eric whispered urgently.

"Don't surrender, Damien, even if he kills me!"

Damien didn't move. He was using all of his strength to keep the sword pointed at Brés.

Brés sneered at him.

"And what gives you leave to defy me? You unlettered bog dwelling chimpanzee?"

"I dwell not in a bog but in a cottage, heathen Fomorian! I may not be skilled in arms or words but this island is fatigued with foreign hordes coming in and telling us to obey them. Your monsters are no different from the Black and Tans that tortured my father! Ireland is a free country and I am a free man!"

Brés was momentarily silenced by this. Some of the people began to slip away while Damien backed towards Oisín who was now barking loudly in anger at Brés. Drawing his own sword, Brés approached Damien.

"Give me the sword, Simian!"

Damien simply spat in Brés' face. Moving swiftly, Eric raised his fist and punched Brés in the face while Damien let the sword fall, chopping through Oisín's leash. With a blood-curdling growl, the dog leapt at Brés who stumbled back under the weight of the massive hound. The Fomorian shook Oisín off and raised his sword to strike him but Eric wrapped his arm around Brés' neck allowing Oisín dodge aside. Seeing Damien still holding the sword, Eric shouted at him.

"Damien!! Get out of there, find Lord Fitzgerald!!!"

Brés wriggled out of Eric's choke and the two struggled together. Brés shoved Eric violently, causing Eric to strike his head off the wall, knocking him out. Damien ran. Brés turned to his followers.

"Go! Kill him and fetch me the sword!! You can kill the other humans later!!"

The Fomorians howled like hyenas as they ran in pursuit of Damien, waving their spears and clubs. Oisín stood over Eric's unconscious body, guarding him. Brés looked at him and shrugged. Swinging around, he left the room to follow the sword.

6

A Battle in Dublin

Damien ran as quickly as he could, hefting the heavy sword. Behind him, the howling grunts followed him like sharks after blood. Some of them threw spears at him as he ran. The grunts stopped then split into three groups as their chieftain directed them with hand signals. One group pursued Damien, the other group went back to kill Eric, and the third went to kill anyone in their path. Eventually, Damien made it into the main hall. He didn't have time to admire the artefacts this time.

Meanwhile, Oisín barked at Eric and licked his face. He kept doing this until Eric let out a groan in pain as he opened his eyes. Slowly, he sat up.

"What? What just happened…"

Then he heard a yell as a grunt came running in while waving a knife. Seeing this, Eric stood up and grabbed onto the grunt's arm and snapped it. He then punched the grunt and knocked him out. Eric looked rather startled as he looked down at the grunt he just knocked out. Another grunt came in roaring and lunged his spear at him. Oisín bit into his leg while Eric grabbed his spear, yanking it out of his hand. Eric plunged the spear into the chest of the grunt, killing him. He then finished off the grunt he had knocked out by jabbing him with the spear. Eric whistled to Oisín.

"Come, boy, let's go and find Quincy and Simon! We need to warn them of what has happened!"

Not too far away, Quincy and Simon were walking together when they heard the howling. Baffled by this, Quincy turned to Simon.

"Did you hear that? You would think a pack of hyenas had somehow made it into the National History Museum....which of course is preposterous considering that there are no hyenas in Dublin."

Quincy laughed as he said this but Simon didn't feel so amused. He reached into his pocket to take out his pistol.

"Those aren't hyenas, Mr. Harker..."

Suddenly, they heard barking and Eric's voice calling.

"Mr. Harker!! Lord Fitzgerald??"

Both men turned around to see Eric running towards them. He stopped, panting as Simon spoke urgently.

"Mr. Trent, what has happened? Why do we hear howling in the distance and where is your assistant, Damien?"

"Gentlemen, I have bad news! This bizarre horned man called Brés, claiming to be the king of the Fomorians showed up. He came looking for the sword and he unleashed savages upon my guests! I thought the Fomorians were a myth!"

Simon's eyes widened.

"You mean they took the sword? Did I not warn you that something like this would happen? You Agarthan fool!"

"No, Simon, no, it is in the hands of Damien, my assistant! Besides, you'll find that not everyone believes in the paranormal so how I was I supposed to know that the myths were real?"

Quincy groaned.

"Oh Eric, you idiot! You left one of the greatest treasures of Ireland in the hands of a common boy..."

At that moment, a horde of grunts began to surround the three men, pointing razor sharp spears and swords at them. They howled and yelled at the three. Eric readied his spear while Simon and Quincy took out their guns, pointing them at the grunts. But before either of them could pull the trigger, the voice of Brés boomed through the noise.

"Wait! Not yet, you scum...I must speak with these humans!"

Eric readied his spear but Brés didn't even look at him this time. He approached Simon and Quincy and spoke to them.

"I understand that the two of you serve a different government, one centred in the neighbouring land of Albion, you are Brutus' folk, you renamed the island Britain when you seized it. Is that right?"

Quincy found his voice.

"Yes, that is right, we call it England now. Though we no longer rule this country we have interests in the North. If you wish to attack Ulster then know that it is under British protection."

Simon looked oddly at Quincy for saying that. Brés smirked as he scratched Quincy's cheek with one of his claws.

"England, yes, Britannia, it was also called. I remember that place for it was the home of the Christian King Arthur. The Roman mortal who stubbornly resisted my conquest. However, he couldn't kill me, for I got in touch with his beautiful half-sister to initiate an....undermining of his kingdom. Englishmen, know that if you make any move against me or my race, I will undermine your society in the worst way possible!"

Rather than responding, Simon and Quincy both opened fire on him. Eric even plunged his spear into him.

But instead of killing Brés, none of these weapons had any effect. They were all dumbstruck as Brés calmly drew the spear out of himself and threw it at Eric's feet. He turned away, sneering.

"Hmmm....poor fools, your mortal weapons cannot kill me. You are not worth my time."

Suddenly, he swung back towards Eric.

"Should have thought of that before you dug up the sword, Lugh!

The calamity that befalls this country will be on your hands!"

Brés laughed as Eric rolled his eyes in frustration. He nodded to the chieftain of his grunts.

"Kill them! Then find the sword!"

Brés stalked away and immediately the grunts howled and charged at them. Eric threw his spear into the chieftain while Quincy and Simon emptied their guns on the grunts, causing them to panic and killing many of them. Soon they ran out of ammo so they were forced to retreat. Racing towards the entrance, Eric gasped.

"Wait a minute! What about Damien? I mean he has the sword!"

Simon shook his head.

"Not now, there are too many of Brés' goblins to find him on our own. We need to find reinforcements first!"

The three made it as far as the room with the Zodiac signs. Two guards waiting there were startled as the three men, followed by a very large dog, bounded into the room.

"Guards! Sound the alert!"

The Guards looked even more confused as Simon added.

"Call the army, do it now!"

"Why? We need a legitimate excuse if we want the support of the army!"

But then they saw the grunts running past the entrance to the main hall, still uttering their unearthly howls. One of the guards grabbed a telephone and with shaking hands, dialled the number for the base at the Phoenix Park.

At the base, an officer was reading a report when the phone rang beside him. Curious, he lifted the receiver.

"Yes, General O'Fahey responding."

His professional calm gave way as he listened to the guard at the other end.

"Tusked monkeys with spears rampaging around the Irish National History Museum?? Is this some sort of joke?"

"We're not making this up, General, we just saw them rampaging and..."

Then O'Fahey heard the howling for himself and realized that this was no joke. He snapped into action.

"Understood, I'll send troops to your location!"

Soon, a troop of riflemen wearing khaki uniforms and Stalhelm helmets left the base in a convoy of trucks.

Back at the museum, Damien was still in the main hall. He was exhausted, afraid and he had a sword that he couldn't use because it was so heavy. In some ways, he longed for the moon to shine its light down on the sword so that it could glow again and kill the Fomorians. He had concealed himself behind a pillar but he couldn't move because the Grunts were searching everywhere for him. All he could do was wait as he heard them chuckling and mumbling to each other in what sounded to Damien's ears like gibberish. He tried to hold up the sword but he trembled under its weight. Then he heard more howling near the entrance which was followed by gunfire and the grunts squealing. Damien felt encouraged because he knew now that help had arrived. But when he moved from behind the pillar he was discovered by a grunt chieftain who growled in his face. At first the creature smiled under its tusks but then acting upon instinct, Damien swung the sword with a strength he didn't know he had, and plunged it into the heart of the grunt, killing it. Gasping with the effort, he pulled the sword out of the body and ran towards the entrance and outside. Desperately looking for a way to escape his pursuers, he spotted a drain. The grunts followed him with glee brandishing spears and knives. Reaching the drain, Damien yanked off the cover so that he could crawl into the sewer.

He was so determined to escape that he didn't even notice the smell as he crawled into the sewer. The current of water was so strong that it dragged him and the sword away from the entrance, wrecking his suit. At first the grunts laughed mockingly, so gleeful about Damien's apparent demise that they didn't even notice he had taken the sword with him. Their glee and joy over their apparent victory was cut violently short by a bullet slicing through a grunt's head, spewing its blood as the creature collapsed on the ground. Seeing this, the grunts howled again and charged in the direction from which the bullet came. They were mowed down mercilessly by riflemen of the Irish army. Any grunts that were still twitching were shot in the head by an officer who ordered.

"Good job, lads! Now round up the bodies and get rid of them. There's no way we're commemorating these bastards."

Eric, Simon and Quincy had followed the soldiers outside. Eric looked around desperately.

"Excuse me gentlemen! Any sign of Damien?"

A rifleman paused.

"Who?"

"Damien O'Laoghaire, he's my assistant, brown haired, sixteen years old, he was carrying a broadsword to protect it from the creatures you just killed."

"Never heard of him, sorry, and I haven't seen any lad of sixteen at all."

A different voice spoke.

"O'Laoghaire, did you just say O'Laoghaire?"

Eric realized the voice came from a sergeant.

"Eh...yes, O'Laoghaire, he's the son of Donal O'Laoghaire..."

"Donal O'Laoghaire, I served under him when I was a raw recruit. He was our commander during the landings of Waterford. Don't tell me you dragged his poor boy into this mess?"

"Well…"

Eric's sentence was cut short by Oisín barking. Curious, Eric turned to see Oisín sniffing at the drain. Quincy looked baffled.

"What is your dog doing, Eric?"

"Before we came here this evening, Damien had petted Oisín. That means Oisín recognises his smell and has just tracked it to the sewers!"

"You mean Damien went into the sewers?"

Eric sighed.

"Yes, and it seems he took the sword with him."

Simon reacted furiously.

"Good God!! That means both Damien and the Claíomh Solais could be anywhere in Dublin! What if he, or worse, the sword, end up in the hands of the IRA?"

Before Eric could answer that, Oisín barked eagerly.

"Well, let's hope that we get to him. If we follow Oisín, we'll be sure to find him. There's only so many places that he can be in this city, and Oisín can show us the way, isn't that right boy?"

Oisín barked and raced off. Eric and Simon followed while Quincy spoke to the officer.

"We'll take it from here sir, thank you for your support."

"Do you think there will be more of these attacks?"

"Alas, we believe so, you should alert the Curragh just in case, so that all your units will be ready, understood?"

"Yes, sir."

Quincy followed the other men through the streets of Dublin, darting past the army trucks that were parked outside the museum and some journalists who had just shown up.

Eric groaned.

"Oh no, we've just attracted unwanted attention!"

Simon cut him off.

"Don't waste your time with them, Eric... let the soldiers deal with them."

Eric could already see the riflemen and their officers leaving the museum. He only hoped that the men were ready for some questions.

Down near Saint's Stephen's Green, it was as if nothing had ever happened and people were just going about their usual activities. Then a drain was lifted as an exhausted and filth covered Damien slowly emerged from the sewer. He pushed the drain back in its place. Unable to walk, he stumbled down onto the path and sat up against the fence that separated the park from the rest of the city. He still clasped the now dirty sword beside him as he lay there. He was in the dangerous position of dozing off in the middle of the street.

Most Dubliners just walked past him as if he weren't even there. He was so filthy from his time in the sewers that one would think that he had come from a Dickensian novel like "Oliver Twist". A boy briefly reached out his hand to him out of curiosity. Damien was so dazed that he almost thought the boy was Seosamh so he reached out his own hand. But then the boy was grabbed by the arm by his mother who pulled him away.

"James! Come on, he's a vagrant, he'll steal us blind!!"

Damien sighed over the helplessness of his situation. He heard the sound of hooves clacking against the cobblestones. The hooves became slower as they came to a stop. Looking up, Damien could see a horse and cart stopping near where he was. The cart driver got off his cart to let his horse drink from the nearby trough. As the horse drank, it began to snort and toss his head from the smell of sewage.

"Hey, hey what is it boy?" asked the driver, surprised.

The driver looked around for the reason for his horse's disturbance. Seeing Damien, he knelt down beside him to tap him on the shoulder. Damien let out a groan and reopened his eyes.

"Where am I??"

"Near Saint Stephen's Green, young man. Who are ye?"

"Damien O'Laoghaire, I'm a museum clerk and I work for the National History Museum."

Baffled, the driver considered the situation, then made a decision.

"Come on, I'm Tom O'Connor, I'll get you to a pub so that you can have a pint."

Standing up, Damien felt a little alarmed.

"Why are ye helping me?"

Tom patted Damien's shoulder.

"Trust me, Damien, I've no interest in your money or that big sword you're looking after. When I see someone like you on the street, I can't just leave them like that. Tell me though, how did a museum clerk like yourself end up smelling like the Dublin sewers?"

Damien put the sword onto the cart beside an array of milk bottles.

"I'm going to be honest with ye, Tom, that is a very long story and it's one ye probably won't believe anyway."

"Ye can tell me on the way then. Up we get!"

Damien climbed onto the cart.

On the other side of Stephen's Green, the three men were still looking for Damien, guided by Oisín. The fact that they had not seen a single sign of Damien since the incident made Eric feel extremely bad about what he had done. He had assured Damien's parents that he would be alright and now there was a high chance that Damien could be dead. It didn't help either, that in digging up the sword from a relatively safe place near a remote Irish town, Eric had just exposed the sword to being up for grabs by earthly and unearthly forces. Shaking his head, he realised Quincy was speaking to him.

"Eric, I think I owe you an apology for trying to bribe you in order to get the sword for Churchill. Your father's old-fashioned sense of honour made me fond of him. It's difficult for the Irish to understand that we are all so frustrated by the War that we will use any measure to make it stop."

Eric nodded solemnly.

"I did something terrible, didn't I, Mr. Harker? I dug up a sword not really understanding what it was or what it meant. Then Brés came here and terrorized my guests. Oh, every time we try to take something for the sake of scholarship, something goes terribly wrong. I might as well be just sweeping streets or delivering milk rather than seeking treasure. The local people always think we are just thieves but we are so much more."

Eric sighed with shame and paused as he put his hand to steady himself against a brick wall. Simon put his hand on his shoulder.

"Well, Eric, be comforted by the fact that if it weren't you, it would be somebody else, nothing stays buried forever. We should thank all the angels and saints that it was you because not only do you have your father's honour but you have connections to us."

Eric tried to smile at this view of the situation.

"Yes, I guess that is a good thing, but Brés is not going to give up because the army shot some of his grunts. He's going to terrorize this entire country including the North. Most people don't believe in faeries so it's not like Ireland's going to have much help from the Allies! He really is the Dark Elf Prince, isn't he?"

Quincy nodded.

"Yes, the Norsemen who came and founded this city even had their own name for the Fomorians: The Dokkalfar, that means the Dark Elves. When the Milesians invaded Ireland, they defeated the

Tuatha De Danann. So scared of men was Brés that he enchanted himself so that no weapon forged by man or Fomorian could kill him. Only weapons forged by the tribe of Danu can kill him."

"Does that include the Claíomh Solais?", Simon asked, brightening.

"Yes, it was a sword held by King Nuada of the Tuatha De Danann himself. It is one of the only Danann weapons left."

"Then we need to find Damien quickly, he has the sword. I brought them both to Dublin and I'm not leaving this city until I find them both."

With that, the three men resumed their search.

Meanwhile the cart was making its way down the cobblestone street as Tom tried to digest the information he had just been given.

"So, let me understand ye, your boss dug up a magic sword and the "fair folk" chased ye into the sewers?"

Damien's eyes widened.

"The "fair folk"?"

"Do you not use that term down the West, Damien?"

"We do, but it doesn't suit the freaks that chased me, Mr. O'Connor. They were ugly and they howled like dogs and they killed anyone that stood in their way."

"I know, Damien. Our grandparents called them the "Fair Folk" in the hope of flattering them so as to stop them from stealing our children. But when the faeries get their hands on ye, they make the Black and Tans look like Christmas elves in comparison."

The thought of that chilled Damien's heart considering his father's experience with the Black and Tans. Eventually they pulled up outside a pub. Pulling on the brake of the cart, they climbed down and entered the pub.

After all the awkwardness of being in high society at the Irish National Museum, Damien was more than relieved to hear a fiddle playing in the warm air of the pub. Walking across the wooden floor, he heard men laughing and sharing stories. Many of them clinked glasses of Guinness or whiskey before gulping it down. Some of the customers were playing darts while a drunk stumbled past Damien and Tom as he made his way to the bathroom. The air was filled with smoke from pipes and cigarettes while two strong bouncers watched the place. The whole atmosphere made Damien feel less homesick because it reminded him of home. In some ways it was even better since the whole place was absolutely full of life. As Damien sat on a stool at the counter, the barkeep asked Tom.

"Well, O'Connor, what can I get ye tonight?"

"Just two glasses of Guinness if you please? One for me and one for the young lad here."

"Who is he?"

"Oh, if I was to tell you his story, you'd think I was drunk already!"

The barkeep went to work filling the two glasses of Guinness. Damien had barely started to drink when he heard a familiar bark and the men around him suddenly went silent. Turning around, Damien saw Oisín come bounding through the crowd to his side. Simon, Eric and Quincy were standing at the door. Eric spoke into the tense atmosphere.

"Gentlemen, I'm looking for a boy of sixteen who has got lost...."

Hearing his English accent, some of the men started to mutter.

"Ah go home Sassenach!! Go back to England. You're not welcome here!!"

Damien was stunned by the viciousness of the whole thing but Eric stayed calm.

"His name is Damien O'Laoghaire, he is my assistant and I promised his mother and father that I'd keep him safe! Now if you can tell me where he is, I will leave this place."

Tom nudged Damien.

"Is he your boss, Damien?"

"Yes...thanks Tom."

"Well maybe you should go to him, before this gets all fiery."

As Damien got off the stool, Tom stood up and snapped at the customers saying.

"Ah would ye all shut up!! This is a place of drinking not rebellion! You all forget that we have our own flag and our own army, even our own government! I could care little about politics and I'm fed up with it echoing across the pub, the mass of us Irishmen want nothing of war. Go to an IRA club if you want to just burn your energy hating King George."

The men all became silent while Damien approached the three men at the door.

"Damien, are you alright?"

"I need a bath boss, if you're wondering what the smell is. I've been in some strange places this evening!"

"I can see that. Come on, young man."

As they left the pub, Tom ran out after them.

"Wait, are ye not forgetting something?"

Tom pulled the sword out of his cart.

"I believe this belongs to you, Sassenach."

Eric took the sword reverently in his hands.

"No, sir, I believe it ultimately belongs to Ireland herself. But I will protect it, thank you."

"Do ye not want a ride home, sir?"

The three men looked at each other. Suddenly weary, they agreed to the ride without saying any more. Tom brought them back to Eric's apartment and got some pounds for his trouble.

7

Vision from Ireland

Back at the apartment, Damien was lying in bed after a hot bath. He let his thoughts drift about all that had just happened to him. Not only was he far from home but he had just discovered that the faeries were real and they were dangerous. They could be anywhere in the night. It took Damien a long time to sleep.

Eric, Simon and Quincy were in the sitting room. Eric poured wine for all of them.

"So, what is our plan? At least the sword is safe with us."

Smoking a cigarette, Quincy replied slowly.

"Well, the obvious plan is that someone has to use that sword to kill Brés. However, as the fable goes it is always easier to say that the bell has to be put on the cat than it is to actually do it. Brés is king of the Fomorians. Not all of his kin are like those monkeys we fought this evening. He has a large army capable of wielding magic to terrible effect.... if his plans succeed his impact on Ireland will out measure any other catastrophe that has ever fallen upon her."

Eric put down his glass and leaned forward.

"Yes, that seems obvious, but won't the army help us? Ireland's defence forces may be small when compared to the force Eisenhower is amassing to invade Europe but it is still considerable. Surely they can help?"

Simon shook his head decisively.

"Ireland's defence forces are defence forces. If we are to stop the Fomorians, we will have to go to the Elf land from where they come. To do that we will need an army that has the capacity to invade Elf Land itself and all the horrors that await there. No mortal army has ever lasted long there, not even the Romans and they were the most successful."

An idea flashed into Eric's mind.

"What about the Pellucidar Expeditionary Corps? You, Mr. Harker, have an army that is not only one of the most advanced but it is an army that is currently not engaged in the preparations for the invasion of Europe by the Allies. That's tons of men and equipment available."

Quincy sighed.

"Yes, we have the capacity to do that, we already have jet engines in most of our aircraft and we have missiles, we even have a fully functioning fleet of the new helicopter machinery, that is only scraping the surface of our current technology..."

At first Eric smiled until Quincy continued.

"But...the Fomorians will be terrorizing the Irish countryside so we would need to set up a forward base of operations in Connacht to react to such attacks. That is where the mounds are which the Fomorians would emerge from. However, that is in Irish territory. Only twenty-three years have passed since the day the treaty was signed in London. From what we saw in that pub, I can only dread the reaction to military convoys coming in from British held Northern Ireland should our intentions not be made very clear."

Eric sighed in frustration.

"Damn it, P.E.C is the only army I know of that is not involved in the war and can help Ireland in her time of need. Do they not realize that with the Elven victory, their quest for independence will be for nothing!"

"You said the only army, Eric?"

Eric looked surprised at Simon's question.

"Well, yes...I mean who else do you speak of?"

"Have you ever heard of the Society of Saint Patrick?"

Eric's pale face flushed with anger.

"You mean the Druids?? Those men tried to have me killed, no worse, they were ready to kill Damien and his little brother Seosamh if I didn't hand over the sword. They were also ready to kill my dog!"

Simon didn't seem concerned by Eric's explosion.

"Eric, if you had a bad experience with the Druids, I am sorry but I assure you that Lord Donacagh has been building up an army numbering in the thousands. They are radical in their belief of a Celtic Christian Ireland and they have even reverse engineered some of our technology. Their zeal strikes fear into the greatest of men, even Rommel fears them! But they are ready to defend Ireland herself from any manifestation of evil, including the Fomorians!"

"But they will kill us, they are fundamentalists, they hate England and the Catholic church! They were ready to kill the O'Laoghaire boys for the sword. They won't hesitate to end our lives?"

Quincy interrupted.

"Not if we bring them "An Claíomh Solais". Eric, they seek to guard the treasures of the Tuatha De Danann. These men are Irishmen steeped in their lore and legends; they understand these treasures in a way that not even I do."

Realizing that Simon and Quincy had a point, Eric calmed down.

"Alright, if we must give them the sword, we will...but let us sleep on this issue. I think we all need a rest."

That night, Eric found it difficult to sleep because even though his body was sore with exhaustion, he was mentally too stimulated to sleep. Questions plagued his mind. Who was Lugh? Why did Brés always call him that? Why did Brés act as if he had met Eric before? Why did he have dreams about these battles with horned grey creatures? Such creatures were obviously the Fomorians but what link did he have to all of this? Sure, his own Agarthan race was linked to the same Tilean species as the Tuatha De Danann that once ruled Ireland but aside from that, what connection did Eric really have with this country? Ever since he had set foot in this country, he constantly got visions and dreams as if someone was trying to communicate with him. Eric tried to sleep but the moment he closed his eyes he felt an icy wind blow against his face.

When he opened his eyes again, he realized that he was in a trance like state as he heard a voice call him by name. As he stumbled in his trance, he could hear the sound of a harp playing in the distance. His vision became less blurry as the sound of the harp became louder. When Eric finally found the source of the music, he was totally speechless and his eyes widened in awe. In front of him and looking down on him from a high place was a gorgeous woman who was so hauntingly beautiful that Eric was firmly convinced that he was in yet another dream. For not only was she taller than any other woman Eric had seen in his life but she wore a dress coloured in a combination of sapphire blue and emerald green that was embroidered with golden yellow symbols. Her skin was as white as the Arctic ice while her orange hair descended in immense, vibrant thick locks beyond her waist. Upon her head was a golden amber crown that was decorated with glowing jewels of different colours ranging from ruby to purple. Her white hands were playing the strings of a golden harp. As Eric came closer to her, her emerald eyes focused firmly on him and she stopped playing.

Unable to take his eyes off her solemn face, he made the effort to speak.

"Who are you? What is your interest in me?"

Her speech was gentle but firm and an echoing rendition of the Irish accent.

"I am known by many names, young man, but my real name is "Danu". When Tilean folk lost their civilization to the Great Flood,

I guided them to this place so that they could have a home. I could only pity such a majestic people who had fallen so far. Mortal men look to me as well. The last human I contacted even helped to write a play about me. They called me names such as "Dark Rosaleen", but their reverence for me was deep."

As she spoke, Eric could hear many different voices echoing and whispering all at once. His jaw dropped in shock because he realised who he was talking to. He wasn't just talking to a mere spirit or witch; he was talking to Ireland herself.

"You....you're Ireland herself. I'm having a conversation with a country...you are one beautiful country, you know that?"

"Yes....I am....so beautiful that many men have died foolishly in my name. Sometimes they loved me more than their own families. But the loss of the Tuatha De Danann permanently severed my capacity to intervene in this world, therefore I can only inspire and influence now, not act as I once did."

As she said this, Danu sadly descended from the place she was and came down to the same level as Eric. He struggled to frame a question for her.

"Danu, if you really are Ireland then please explain how ever since I set foot on your land, I have had dreams, dreams that are as strong as memories. They help guide me more effectively than the maps men have made of you. Tell me Great Goddess, is it you who sends these visions?"

"Yes, I do, for it is the only way I can truly communicate with people within the physical realm. King Brés waited long for the opportunity to strike this land....and the Claíomh Solais is the only weapon left that could slay him."

Eric grew even more confused.

"But you are Ireland? Why me? I may be of Agarthan blood but I am an Englishman who grew up in France....many men of great bravery have been born native to your soil; I am a complete outsider. No matter how I try to adapt, I would never be truly Irish. All I did was steal the Claíomh Solais! I'm the reason Brés is on the warpath, why have you chosen me...explain to me, Great Goddess?"

Putting her hands on Eric's shoulders suddenly made him feel much warmer as she answered him. "If that is so, then that is why you must stop him. You have more in common with me than you think. Under another name, you saved Ireland from the Fomorians under King Balor."

"Wait, a different name?"

Suddenly, he realised that Danu was starting to fade away. Horrified, Eric cried out.

"Wait? Danu? What am I really? Danu, wait! What is my other name, don't go!"

Danu's voice was fading too.

"I can only last in this form for so long, Eric....I will meet you again, young man."

"But..."

Danu faded away and slowly everything started to blur causing Eric to stumble backwards in panic. Suddenly all went dark for a while.

Eric was deeply asleep when there was a knock on the door. He could hear the bustling sounds of the city outside as he opened his eyes. Church bells rang across the city alongside the noise of vehicles, drills, horse hooves clacking against the cobblestone roads as well as the sound of people chatting and shouting to each other. Eric opened his eyes wider and realized that the day had come. Yet despite this, he didn't have the urge to move from his bed until he heard the knock again. He groaned.

"Yes? Come in?"

The door opened and Oisín came in panting followed by Damien with a tray of toast and tea. He was clean and tidy, dressed in his original clothes. Eric sat up and accepted the tray.

"Ah, hello Damien, back in your ordinary clothes, are you?"

"Well sir, an evening suit may symbolize status but it's not much use in the mud or the rain of Connacht. Anyway, boss, Lord Fitzgerald asked if I could wake ye up and get you some breakfast."

Munching on the toast, Eric began to feel much better.

Thank you, Damien. Now could you please tell me what time it is?"

"It's seven o'clock now, boss. Lord Fitzgerald and Mr. Harker said we need to get to Dublin airport by eight o'clock where we are to rendezvous with our pilot who will fly us to the Druids."

"What?? Oh no!! Hold on, Damien, I'll get myself dressed as soon as possible!"

A taxi took them to the airport. Oísin snoozed on the floor, his head on his paws. On the way, Eric was reading a newspaper that he had brought with him. He read out the headline.

"Army in combat with Ape-men? Are these ape-men faeries or just Yahoos? Horned man disrupted the archaeological presentation of a glowing sword!"

He continued reading to himself.

"Did our famous treasure, "an Claíomh Solais" end up in Dublin Sewers? English archaeologist stealing our treasures?"

Eric rolled his eyes and groaned.

"We're all over the front page. Whatever hope we had of secrecy is gone because of the press's need for sensationalised versions of information."

"Ahh...that's not surprising, my trip in the sewers is going to be splattered all over the press in order to drown out all discussion about the economic situation of Ireland."

"Does your family read the press, Damien?"

"No, I hate newspapers, they always made my father angry. It made the little ones upset and my poor mother had to throw out any newspapers that were brought into the house."

"Good, you are not impoverished if you don't read papers. If you're literate, always read a book or an academic article, not a newspaper. Reading articles in Paris's library is how I found about the Claíomh Solais."

At the airport, Eric unloaded the suitcases, including the one that carried the sword. Their new objective was to take it to the Druids. Simon paid the driver. Damien had been puzzling over the absence of Quincy Harker.

"Lord Fitzgerald? Where is Mr. Harker? Why didn't he come with us?"

"Quincy left this morning at seven thirty."

"What? What for?"

"He headed for the Dáil; he's hoping to persuade the Irish government to allow P.E.C operations in Connacht."

"So, who are we waiting for now, Lord Fitzgerald?"

"A friend apparently, he's going to fly us to the Druids."

Suddenly, they heard a voice that was familiar to both Eric and Simon.

"Well, hello lads!! You look well dressed for this occasion!"

Eric and Simon turned around to see a man dressed in a leather jacket; a man they recognised and whose eccentricities were not curbed by his aging body. Both Simon and Eric looked delighted.

"Phil? My God, if it is not Phillip George Rodgers? The git who was able to earn his place in the Pellucidar Expeditionary Air Corps by slaying a dragon. What happened to your hair, it is getting grey?"

Phil chuckled. His hair was getting increasingly grey and his skin was starting to wrinkle. "Alas, good sir, I got older, age comes to us all, doesn't it Simon?"

"Yes, but I retired because of my age, you are not only older but still in active service?"

"Of course, I am, but I will admit, I'm not the ace I was in 1918. Age has somehow interfered with my capacity, but I will go down as a pilot rather than rot away like some old king on his deathbed!"

The two laughed and Phil then turned to Eric smiling.

"Look at you, Eric, time loves your species, doesn't it?"

"I guess it does."

"Still, you've changed a lot since you were nine, a lot less wimpy than you were then."

"Well, you have to toughen up unless you want to be a corpse."

Phil leaned down and patted Oísin's head.

"So, you're still around too, are you?"

The two men laughed as Oísin barked in reply. Then Phil noticed Damien who faced him and tried to smile.

Seeing Damien, Phil asked.

"Well, well, who is this little bunny rabbit?"

Damien's eyes widened and his cheeks grew crimson.

"Damien, sir, Damien O'Laoghaire. I'm from County Mayo..."

"Oh yes, I can figure that out from the accent. Gentlemen, why is he here?"

Damien felt a sting in his heart when Phil asked that. Probably because, deep down, he was wondering the same thing. However, Eric stood up for him immediately.

"Now, now, Phil, have some respect for this young gentleman. Damien O'Laoghaire is temporarily employed as my personal assistant. He helped me find the "Sword of Light" and protected it from the Fomorians. If anything, he proves that you don't need harsh boarding schools and pampered universities to forge a great mind."

Hearing this made Damien feel much better. Phil nodded thoughtfully.

"Very well... how comfortable are you in an aircraft?"

"Eh....until this point, I have spent most of my life in a town with little electricity. I've never been in a plane before."

Phil put his hand on Damien's shoulder.

"Well come along my little bunny rabbit... I'll give you your first dose."

Damien felt strangely nervous as he followed Phil. Simon and Eric walked behind.

"Phil hasn't changed much since his Victorian upbringing, has he?"

"I hope he doesn't talk like that to the Druids."

"Don't worry, Phil is smarter than to talk down to men with guns."

The group reached a field that wasn't too far from the main airstrip. Parked in this field was a large four engine aeroplane that was khaki and patterned with RAF insignia but had the red cross of Saint George to signify it was a monster fighting aircraft. It had a few machine gun turrets on it, making Damien wonder how Phil was able to sneak such a plane into Ireland.Some ground crew dressed in khaki outfits and baseball caps were tending to the plane's maintenance. Phil was visibly proud as he turned back to his passengers.

"Well, gentlemen, how do you like it?"

"A Lancaster I presume, is it?"

"Yes, that is the model, Eric, but it's equipped with a kitchen, a shower, even bunk beds instead of bombs. Most importantly for this young fellow..."

Phil turned to Damien and winked.

"There is a toilet for those who are flying for the first time."

He bounded up the steps of the plane.

"Well come on gentlemen, chop, chop!"

The men boarded the plane after Phil and his crew. Damien was the last to get in. He couldn't believe himself as he entered the metallic hull of the plane. As a boy who grew up in a village with lanterns and fireplaces, he never thought he would get in a plane, especially a plane as modern as this. However, his excitement turned to hostility as he saw crows circling in the air outside, croaking. Oisín growled as he saw them. He followed the others past some oxygen tanks which were attached to the plane via tubes and sat down beside Eric as Phil climbed into the cockpit. Following orders from the crew, Damien buckled his seatbelt and tried to relax.

Outside the crows observed the plane but their harsh croaks were soon drowned out first by a bang, followed by the sputtering engines all going on one by one. The propellers started to spin as the plane started to move as fast as possible across the field before eventually taking off and soaring up into the cloudy sky. Damien looked down at the floor during the bumpy journey as the plane went higher into the air. By this time, Damien had started to feel immensely queasy and he started to recoil as if about to throw up. Sitting across from him, Simon noticed immediately.

"Damien? Eric, something's wrong with Damien!"

Eric turned to look at his young assistant.

"Damien? Are you alright?"

"Eh...sir....I'm sorry but I think I'm about to t..."

Damien felt an immense pressure and he unbuckled himself, rising from his seat only to stumble down onto the floor. Simon called to Phil.

"Phil! Phil! We need some help here, our lad from Mayo is in trouble."

Phil turned over control of the aircraft to his co-pilot.

"Stephen, keep your hands on the controls! I'm going to find out what's going on!"

"Yes, sir!"

Arriving into the cargo hold he saw Damien on the ground, with the other two bending over him.

"Phil, where is the bathroom? It's his first flight so..."

"I can figure that out, it happens to everyone.... come on, give him to me!"

Phil took Damien and maneuvered him to the toilet so that he could throw up there. When that was done, he opened the door again, and saw Damien panting and looking miserable. Seeing Damien like this melted any ill-feeling he had towards the youth.

"Are you alright, there, O'Laoghaire?"

"I'm sorry... I thought I could h..."

"Get up, there's nothing to be sorry about. It's alright."

Damien's eyes looked red and Phil put his hand on his shoulder.

"Listen, it happened to me, it might have even happened to the Red Baron. Now, we'll soon be flying at a normal speed and you can see your country as God sees it. Okay?"

Damien nodded but he was secretly terrified that he'd get sick again. Phil patted him on the back.

"Come, I'll get you your bunk so that you can sleep... if it makes you comfortable you didn't leave much of a mess."

Damien followed Phil to the bunks. As he looked down, he could see the ground below. Below lay immense cultivated and green fields patterned with roads, cities and towns. Looking down gave Damien a strange sense of awe as he saw Ireland like a bird sees it. There were so many towns and villages not too different from his own. For now, the plane flew in the cloudy sky as it headed for its destination, a Druid fort near the Anglo-Irish Border.

8

The Journey to the Druids Begins

In the dark, twisted world of Elfland, Brés looked out from the bramble-infested ruin that was his fortress. In Elfland, not much grew except for brambles and leafless trees, forcing creatures to fight and kill each other for food. It was perpetually night-time in Elfland as there was no sun, only a moon which left the land barren, dull and twisted. When one looked up, dragons could be seen flying against the dark sky.

In this ancient world of the Fomorians, dark magic was fuelled by death. This was achieved through the ritual sacrifice of anyone they saw fit, including human infants whom they stole from Ireland. Dotted across Elfland were portals that could open into different points of Ireland. Unlike the mounds on the other side, these portals were made of twisted and gnarled branches that formed a circle. It was out of one of these portals that a crow came as it flew over the dead landscape, searching for Brés.

Brés retreated to his throne and slumped down as he thought to himself. The crow perched itself on the wall. Multiple Fomorian warriors stood guard in the area around the throne. Brés addressed the newcomer.

"What news of the surface? Has the sword been taken from the humans?"

"Your grunts have failed you, sire! Men's weapons have become considerable, sire!"

Already furious with the knowledge that An Claíomh Solais was still among the humans, Brés could not resist his curiosity.

"In what way??"

"With these strange lances that shoot metal, the human soldiers were able to annihilate your grunts! I have seen them amass a variety of contraptions from their cauldrons of smoke and steel. These monstrosities which they call "machines" can bring down even the most formidable creatures of Elf Land…"

"Enough!! There's nothing that enrages us Fomorians more than knowledge that those hairless apes we call "men" are building a thriving society more powerful than possibly even the Tuatha De Danann while we Fomorians, a superior race, starve and live on scraps in this forsaken place. Tell me, crow, where is the sword?"

The crow preened himself before responding.

"The sword is being transported by a flying machine to the Druids, sir! The Society of Saint Patrick is possibly the deadliest obstacle to our domination of the island. But they do have the cauldron of Dagda, another of the great treasures of Ireland. As we know such a cauldron is a cauldron of plenty and can even bring back life, sire!"

"Of what use is this knowledge to me, creature?"

"The sword of light is still on its way and the cauldron, if stolen, can be used to resurrect Balor and his army! But I warn you, the humans will do anything to stop you from getting either artefact!"

Brés stood up and raised his clawed hands in glee.

"If there is one thing that hasn't changed about men it is their bellies and their need to consume! You, crow, understand their society better than any other creature from Elfland. Inform the witches, goblins, gremlins and all other Fomorian folk. Tell them to attack their farms and their towns, anything that sustains them. Their weapons and machines are only so strong when their wielders are hungry and weak in spirit! Send the word!"

"We will do as you ask, my Lord!"

The crow fluttered off while Brés turned to his guards.

"Bring me my magic crystal! I would like to observe Lugh and his human friends!"

The warrior bowed and then went off to find the crystal.

Back in Ireland, not too far from Damien's village, night was settling but some of the villagers from his hometown were still digging for turf in the nearby bog. As a villager plunged his long spade known as a "slean" into the bog, he spoke to his friend in Irish.

"By the way, Manus, do we have any word from Damien O'Laoghaire? He went to Dublin, didn't he?"

Manus, exhausted from the hard digging he was doing in the bog had little time to think about Damien.

"Yeah, he did, he went with the English archaeologist to Dublin, Cillian."

"Ah, the lucky bastard, living like a prince in the "Pale" while we're still shovelling peat to light our homes…"

Suddenly the horse started to snort and rear. The two men stopped what they were doing. Manus turned to Cillian.

"What the hell is wrong with this fella? He's normally very calm, isn't he?"

"I know but look at what is going on in the bog!"

Many of the other villagers had stopped to stare as a fog crept over the bog. Slowly but surely, it crept towards them. Manus was puzzled.

"By the Virgin mother, what sort of fog is this?"

"I don't know, Manus, but it certainly isn't Irish weather…"

Suddenly, an ear-splitting scream echoed across the bog causing all the villagers to cluster around the cart where their only light, a small lantern, rested. The wailing continued across the bog and the villagers started to panic. They were chilled to the bone by the sound and Cillian could now see the figure of a cloaked and hooded old woman in the distance. As the scream was heard again, the villagers began to panic.

"It's the wail of the banshee, it screams to warn ye all of your deaths or the death of your relatives! If we do not flee, we will be destroyed entirely!"

Then Cillian noticed movement in the bog. Curious he reached out with his slean only to feel an immense pressure that seemed strong enough to tug at him. Horrified, he saw a rotting skeletal hand grabbing at the tip of his slean. Cillian tried to pull the slean away from it, but he could not wrest it from the hand's grasp. The hand submerged, pulling the slean with it, and in turn pulling Cillian after it. Slowly he was pulled in, screaming for help, as another hand from the bog grabbed onto his arm.

The villagers rushed over to help Cillian but they were powerless to prevent him from being dragged into the bog. Manus could only look on helplessly as he saw Cillian's shoes finally submerge below the bog. Terrified, the villagers started to run as bursting out of the bog came corpses who though preserved by the bog had shrunken bodies. They emerged slumping from the bog and groaned as they reached out their bony hands. As they saw this, a villager screamed. "Lord save us! It's the day of judgement!"

"Get to the church! Ask the priest for salvation!"

Without thinking, Manus jumped onto the cart. He took up the lantern and threw it at the undead bog bodies, burning some of them and buying some of the other villagers time to climb up after him. Manus yanked at the reins causing the horse to go running at full speed. But some were left behind, doomed to be torn apart by the dead.

Observing the whole scene was a troop of Fomorians, staring unemotionally as they saw the chaos that they created. A Fomorian noted the fleeing cart, she snarled as she raised her bow and pulled back the string to loosen an arrow but her chieftain stopped her.

"No! Let them spread the news and be afraid!"

"But they'll summon warriors!"

"No, the fear must spread, their worship has given them a guilt complex that we can exploit to damage their morale."

The Fomorian lowered her bow but allowed herself a smirk at the chaos they had already caused among the humans.

Not too far from the bog, a train was making its way along the tracks. Little did they know but watching the train was a troop of Fomorians riding horned horses that were twice the size of an average horse. Such creatures were the Pucas. Seeing the train, the chieftain raised his spear and shouted to his warriors to signal to them to advance. It was clear that war had been declared.

Back up in the plane as it made its journey through the night, Eric and Simon were in the cargo hold even though it was night. As they drank coffee, Eric put a question to Simon.

"Lord Fitzgerald? Simon? May I ask you something?"

"Go ahead?"

"Who beat the Fomorians?"

Simon took another gulp from his mug.

"Lugh. Lugh was grandson of the Fomorian King Balor himself. He was a warrior prince of the Tuatha De Danann who led the armies of the tribe of Danu into battle. You see Brés was also half Fomorian and half Danann, but he ruled the Danann with cruelty so the Tuatha De Danann rebelled. At first, this rebellion wasn't too troubling for the Fomorians but once Lugh took control, they became more coordinated. Brés went to Balor for assistance and Balor led a large army of giant monsters to try and crush Lugh's revolt..."

"Did he succeed?"

"No, he didn't. The Tuatha De Danann reclaimed Ireland and Lugh killed Balor while banishing Brés to Elf-land from where Brés came from. Does that answer your question, Eric?"

But Eric was in shock at hearing the name "Lugh".

"Lugh? Lugh? But that was the name Brés called me in Dublin. Look, ever since I've been in Ireland, I've been getting these vivid dreams. Firstly, the dreams depicted battles between what looked like towering Celts battling monsters, then one of me slaying this eldritch monstrosity. And then I got a vision of Ireland herself in the form of a most gorgeous woman."

Eric was expecting to be laughed at for saying that last part but Simon seemed startled.

"A woman? That was an Aisling you got."

"An "Aisling", what is that?"

"The mother goddess of the Tuatha De Danann is Danu. The daughter of Mother Earth, she became the goddess of Ireland. Though both feared and worshipped by the Tuatha De Danann, she lost her power after the Milesians came. She survived by ascending to a different plane of existence in which she can only interact in dreams. When Cromwell's soldiers took over Ireland, Danu started to appear in the hearts of poets and rebellious leaders, in these visions called "Aislings". She called on them to free Ireland from the British Empire. Even Yeats believed he had contact with her."

Hearing this, Eric felt confused and also felt an icy chill go up his spine.

"But I'm English, Simon and grew up in Paris. Yet she says that under a different name, I saved Ireland from the Fomorians. Lord, what if I am Lugh? What if I am a reincarnated version of Lugh himself?"

"Potentially, that would explain why you found the sword but that means little to the mission. We still bring the Claíomh Solais to the Druids."

"But Simon, do you not understand, this means everything to me, this means I'm linked to Ireland, that I'm the one to save Ireland from the Fomorians again. I'm linked to this country and I never knew it. My parents never knew it."

Simon cut across Eric's excitement.

"Listen, Eric, what matters is that Ireland is fighting a war with something most of the world sees as a children's fairy tale. There will be no help coming from the Allied governments or any other regular government. Ireland will need all the help it can get. Whether that help be the Druids, P.E.C or most importantly you and the Claíomh Solais, Ireland will need help regardless of who it comes from, understood?"

Still looking dazed , Eric walked off deeper into the cargo bay to find the sword. Damien came into the hold and sat down in front of Simon.

"What's up with Eric, Lord Fitzgerald?"

"He's having a bit of a dilemma; he's been having visions from Ireland herself. An Aisling, I believe."

"Interesting, I never had an Aisling vision before, lucky Eric."

Simon snapped.

"Really! All too often have that Goddess' visions motivated men to inflict carnage in her name. Even Yeats when he transmitted her power to the stage in his and Lady Gregory's play "Cathleen Ni Houlihan" regretted it, wondering if his play sent out men to die in the Rising."

"Ye are of the Anglo-Irish are ye not?"

"I was, but like so many others, I joined the army in the last Great War and fought for Home Rule. I was naive back then. I was too dumb to realise that Pearse and his sycophants would launch their rising when so many of us were at war. Ireland changed utterly after that..."

"Yet ye fought for the Crown? My father and his mates talked of all of ye lot as traitors and backstabbers for that."

Simon's eyes widened.

"Traitors and backstabbers?? Us? They call us the traitors and backstabbers. Of course, I fought for the Crown! We fought for the promise of Home Rule! We would have gotten it if Pearse hadn't launched his rising! I hated Ireland after that, Ireland's freedom meant nothing to me after that! For Ireland I was an enemy but to England I was a war hero and monster fighter."

Damien looked saddened upon hearing that.

"What made you hate your own people so much? My father told me to hate men like ye."

Simon took out a cigarette, smoked and began to smoke.

"Hate? I hated Irish freedom when I walked the streets of Dublin and saw babies scattered in their prams along the pavements, infants with bullets in them. Why? Because they were caught in the crossfire. When I saw the rebels shoot women and children, I shot them in cold blood. I didn't care that they were lads of sixteen or nineteen, I just cared that they stabbed our backs when we tried to secure them independence and home rule through service and they called us the traitors?"

Damien gasped.

"You were there? You were there in Easter 1916?"

"I was, and all I remember was the screams of the innocent when they got shot or blown up. For it was that day that God taught me to think for myself and not just blindly follow orders, even if you are on the receiving end of a bullet."

"But if ye hate Ireland so much, then why do ye help us out now? Brés is not much of a threat to England, is he?"

"Damien, when Brés' monsters win and take Dublin, we will hear the screams of children on the pavements once more. That is something I never want to happen again. I have no time for Irish politics…"

He reached out and put his hand on Damien's shoulder.

"But I have time for the Irish people."

Damien's heart warmed slightly.

"I had no time for Republicans either, all I wanted was a job so that I could feed my family properly. It's why I was digging for the sword in the first place. I certainly got more than that..."

Simon smiled at him.

"Wouldn't mind meeting your father, see what he's like. Already it seems that he raised you right."

Damien smiled back as he heard those words.

9

Nightmare

Eric paused among the cargo crates feeling as if a heavy weight was being pressed against his chest. His heart was conflicted by the new knowledge he had just gained. He wasn't just from Agartha, but he was certain now that he was a reincarnated Lugh. That wouldn't just make him the last Agarthan but also the last of the Tribe of Danu. This made Danu's connection to him all the more poignant. On the verge of tears, he breathed deeply and mustered his strength. He pressed his hand to his chest, listening to his slow but deep heartbeat. It thumped like a drum and it was the type of heartbeat that all of his species had. It helped to comfort him. He closed his eyes as he listened, so he didn't notice Phil coming in to make the daily routine inspection of his plane until he spoke.

"Still feeling that heartbeat of yours, Eric?"

Eric nodded.

"It was something my mother told me to do when I was distressed or upset. It was a reminder that all my ancestors were still with me even if they were all dead. I hope your species never gets to know what it is like to be the last of your race."

"Oh, Eric, what's got you all messed up this time? Is it the way I spoke to your young assistant?"

"Of course not, Phil, but come, I need to show you something."

Eric beckoned Phil to come over and opened the suitcase. As he watched, Phil gasped as Eric lifted out the enormous sword that was the "Claíomh Solais". Phil looked in amazement as he saw the sword glow in a golden amber colour.

"What in the name of God? Is this the sword of light? The magic sword you are bringing to the Druids?"

"Yes," Eric spoke sternly.

"It is the only weapon that can kill the Fomorian King Brés. Until we are in battle, the sword must not be exposed to the light of the sun or the moon."

Phil looked at him thoughtfully.

"Well, Eric, you are one lucky bastard to be able to wield that! Why are you so conflicted?"

Eric sighed as he placed the sword as gently as possible back in the suitcase.

"Phil, I need to tell you something but the problem is that I don't think you will believe it. Will you?"

"Oh Eric, come on, I've seen dragons, the undead; I work for an organisation established by the man who killed Count Dracula himself; I've seen merfolk and even Hollow Earth with my own two eyes! Now I've seen one of the four treasures of Ireland! Eric my boy, what is there not to believe?"

"Phil, I'm a reincarnation of Lugh, the chieftain who led the Tribe of Danu into battle against the Fomorians. I've spoken with Ireland herself. She sends me visions about what is happening. It's how I found the sword. And now, we must defeat Brés, the Fomorian King."

Phil widened his eyes. It took him a while to get his head around the fact that the man standing in front of him was essentially the reincarnation of a pagan god. Eventually he found his voice.

"You get visions from Mother Ireland, do you? Lucky boy, be glad you're not married if that is the case…"

"Why?"

"Because If I've got my myths right, you won't just fight for her, you won't just serve her, you will die in her name! Now come on! Get some sleep, you'll need it for the journey ahead."

Some hours later, Eric was fast asleep when suddenly, he had another vision. This vision portrayed the macabre image of a locomotive on fire as screeching, winged creatures flew over it. Alongside the burning train was a horde of horned horses galloping, carrying the Fomorians on their backs. As the Fomorians rode past the train and its burning carriages, they raised their brambled bows and spears. They yelled out war cries as the locomotive exploded into flames.

Eric awoke with a gasp. He stumbled off his bunk bed and slammed against the ground. The noise woke both Simon and Damien. Getting out of their beds, they came over to Eric as he lay groaning on the floor.

"You alright?"

"Eh, yes, I should be...oh God that hurt."

"What happened?"

As Eric recovered his senses, Damien went over to the window and looked down on the land below. His eyes widened with fright.

"Lads? Lads!! Ye got to see this! Look!"

Joining Damien at the window, Eric gasped at the sight of a fire blazing far below them.

"Oh no, the train really was attacked. I saw it in yet another vision! Danu must have sent it to me."

Eric scrambled away from the sleeping quarters and rushed through the plane towards the cockpit. Damien cried out behind him.

"Eric? Boss? Was that the route we used to go to Dublin? What if that means......"

Phil's co-pilot Stephen came out to meet Eric with a face that had urgency written all over it.

"Have you listened to the radio?"

Eric's face manifested a sense of dread.

"Eh, no, but we've just seen a train go on fire. What's on the radio?"

"The Taoiseach has ordered a full mobilization of the army! There have been attacks reported all over the country! Farms have been burnt, trains sacked, villagers dragged into bogs. We must get to the Druids and alert them to the crisis."

Eric's jaw dropped in horror and a sense of guilt invaded his heart.

"Oh no, all this because of the sword of light. God, I do hope that the Druids are out there already fighting the Fomorians. Full speed ahead, Stephen, we need to get there as soon as possible!!"

He turned to find Damien standing behind him.

"Wait, so there are attacks all over the country, does that mean my hometown has been attacked??"

Eric hesitated.

"I don't know, none of us know."

Damien gasped with the effort not to cry.

"But we have to go back to my home! What if it gets sacked by the Fomorians?? I can only imagine what my little brother and sister are going through, they'll be terrified of the creatures! My father's mutilated hand means that he's not able to handle a rifle properly. Without help, the village can only last so long without any support."

"Damien O'Laoghaire, we are not in any position to help your people! This plane is poorly armed, we need a proper army and we are going to the Society of Saint Patrick as planned, is that understood??"

"The society of Saint Patrick?? You mean the same batch of bastards who tried to kill me and my brother in order to blackmail ye into giving them the sword? They're our allies all of a sudden?"

"Damien, please! You've got to trust us! The Druids are the only army native to Ireland that can fight the Fomorians properly! They also have more knowledge about them than even P.E.C has…"

"Look, I get that, Boss, but what if by the time, we get to the Druids, MY VILLAGE IS BURNING LIKE A PILE OF TURF!!"

"Damien, that won't happen…. DAMIEN!!"

Damien stormed back through the hull as if to find the arsenal. Eric breathed heavily with guilt and frustration. Simon had been observing the exchange between them.

"Well, Eric, he has a point. These attacks seem to deliberately target civilians. It's as if Brés is trying to inflict a war of attrition on us."

Eric shook his head in frustration.

"At this current time, we will be outnumbered on our own! Look if it eases the boy's mind, I know the coordinates of his hometown."

"What do you want me to do?"

Eric gave Simon the ordnance survey map which had the coordinates of Damien's hometown.

"Take these coordinates, get to the radio and contact the Curragh. Send these coordinates to the army. Hopefully, they will send a unit to help the village. Understand?"

"Understood."

Simon took the coordinates and went into the cockpit to find the radio.

Meanwhile, Damien continued to look down at the burning train. He then heard gunfire from below as shapes that looked to be armoured cars moved in. As well, he could see what looked to be guns shooting at the Fomorians below. Eric came up behind him.

"Damien…Damien…you've got to understand…"

"That we don't have the means at this moment? I know we don't, Mr. Trent, I'm sorry…I shouldn't have snapped at you like that. I probably sound like a selfish bastard to ye…It's just that I fear for my village. It's my home, my family, my people's way of life revolves around it…it's all that I've known before I met ye…"

Eric put his hand on Damien's shoulder.

"I know, trust me, Damien, the fear of losing everything you knew is something we can all relate to quite easily. We've sent word to the army to protect as many towns and villages as possible throughout Ireland. It's alright."

Eric and Damien hugged each other. Below, the sound of gunfire and machine gun rattles continued, accompanied by the sounds of planes swooping in to attack.

For down below, the Irish army had just engaged the Fomorian force. Despite suffering several losses, the army was able to drive back the Fomorian horde.

10

The War begins to Escalate

Back in Dublin, it seemed that little had happened. To an outside view one would not imagine that the Irish State was now locked in a war with the Fomorians. However, at the gates of the Dáil was a protest. The protesters were protesting over food shortages, holding up their banners standing in front of the guards. Quincy had to navigate through this crowd which wasn't easy as the protestors were hungry and tired. He managed to get through with the help of a guard who then allowed him to enter through the gates.

"Sir? The British ambassador in Dublin contacted the Taoiseach to inform him that I was coming. Did he receive the message?"

"Currently, Mr. Harker, he is in conversation with both Sean Lemass and Bishop Mc Quaid over what to do in Ireland. You've chosen an interesting time to come, when the country could be on the verge of yet another great famine, possibly even worse than the one in 1847!"

"Yes, I'm aware of that, but this famine will not be caused by blight. Farms were being attacked and burnt all over Ireland last night!"

"In every county in the country?"

"Yes, territories in the North have been attacked too. The British government has become alarmed and is starting to take action."

As they walked through the corridor, the guard put his thoughts into words.

"Dear God! The whole economy could be on the verge of collapse! The IRA couldn't have pulled that off, could they?"

"Oh no, the threat that menaces your people is far more severe. There is no way they could pull off a stunt as deadly as what is happening now. I must speak with your Prime Minister."

The guard pointed down the corridor.

"The office of the Taoiseach is down there."

"Thank you, sir."

Quincy found the room and entered. De Valera was sitting at his desk with the Irish Tricolour on either side of his chair. Sitting in front of him was Sean Lemass. Quincy approached slowly as De Valera was speaking.

"Well, it is clear that we have been attacked by some enemy of unknown origins. Who this enemy is we can't guess but what is clear is that they have done considerable damage to the well-being of the State. Farms have been burnt, babies stolen to be sacrificed in gruesome rituals, men dragged into bogs, we've had reports of rape. Already we can tell that these creatures have no moral boundaries. Now, the army has already been fully mobilized to fight the threat but we are merely a defence force. Mr. Lemass, explain what solutions you can propose to sustain our state?"

Lemass sighed in frustration as he replied.

"Mr. De Valera, with the state that our economy is in at this present time, there is only so much that we can do…"

He turned to his blackboard and pointed to the drawings he had on it. The drawings depicted a map of Ireland with different routes as he said.

"Firstly, if there is any good news it's that we know there is a pattern in these attacks. They happen at night and the creatures emerge from pre-Celtic burial mounds around the country. That makes our countryside the primary target. Two, we know that they can be killed with bullets and shells but three, these attacks aren't just mere raiding parties. These are well targeted attacks on unarmed people."

Indicating the board, Lemass continued sternly.

"Gentlemen, I have been able to work out two possible responses. One is that we put the whole state on lockdown, shut down every route and encourage self-sufficiency within these counties till the threat is dealt with and the attacks stop coming. As the attacks mostly happen at night, we will impose curfews across the country. However, a lockdown will only make the lives of the people more miserable than they were when the Emergency began. The second option is that we maintain supply routes under armed guards. Train routes will be kept open to bring in supplies and medical equipment. Rumours have spread among the villagers that what we face is the fair folk. That means, if I got my mythology right, they can't cross running water such as rivers."

"How does that benefit us, Mr. Lemass?"

"With our barges, we could potentially pull off a permanent supply chain that will be safe and secure from their attacks. All we have to do is mount riflemen, machine guns and flack cannons onto these barges and they should be relatively safe. Our air force can also ferry supplies from the ports to the cities. We have a lot of rivers in this country, we better start using them."

De Valera frowned.

"Do you think the army is ready for a perpetual war against the fair folk?"

Sean Lemass paused, then took a deep breath.

"I'm going to be blunt with you and I know you won't like this answer but probably not. The army can defend our people for now, but we don't know how many waves there will be. Even implementing my proposals is going to strain the budget and we might be forced to increase our foreign borrowing. It's not a war we can fight alone. We need to contact either Mr. Roosevelt or Mr. Churchill for…"

De Valera cut across him.

"No! No! We will stay neutral in their war. Churchill will use this operation as a way to gain dominance over Ireland. Even if these faeries are in the Dáil with a knife against my throat, I WILL

NOT GET OUR COUNTRY DRAGGED INTO THE SECOND WORLD WAR!!"

As he heard this, Quincy could contain himself no longer so he said.

"Forgive me for interrupting your council gentlemen, but you may have little choice but to call for help."

Both men turned to face Quincy.

"Who are you?" demanded De Valera, "What business does an Englishman such as yourself have in disrupting our council to tell us how to defend our country?"

"Apologies, gentlemen for any rudeness I have committed but my name is Quincy Harker. I am in charge of the Pellucidar Expeditionary Corps, the most powerful army of Christendom that is dedicated to fighting the supernatural. I have come to tell you all that you are not alone in this battle."

There was a pause. Then De Valera spoke in a more moderate tone.

"I am listening! What do you mean?"

"Firstly, my P.E.C army is ready to move in from the North. Due to faery attacks in Ulster against Unionist property, Mr. Churchill requested us to send troops from our base in Scraw-Fell to deal with the problem. An individual P.E.C battalion has three times the fire power of government armies, even the Wehrmacht. All you need to do, Taoiseach, is to give me the authorization to send in soldiers. My finest commander, an American by the name of Francis Bastian O'Connell, will lead them."

The two men muttered to each other while Quincy continued.

"And if you are not comfortable with foreigners in your country, there is always the Druids. Though they have a bone to pick with the Church of Rome and are radical nationalists, they are very effective at killing monsters. Rumours have spread among your citizens that they are already out doing battle with the Fomorians. I have a delegation of men flying over Irish skies at this very moment to meet them and form a military alliance…"

De Valera clearly alarmed, responded.

"The Druids cannot be trusted! They may call themselves Christian but they are increasingly becoming pagan monarchists and have no loyalty to this government. I already thwarted a totalitarian take over at the hands of O'Duffy, Mr. Harker, what makes you think that Lord Donacagh won't pull off a similar stunt…"

"Well, in that case, I offer the services of the Pellucidar Expeditionary Corps once again. My father deliberately set up such an army for a situation like this."

"Your father, the great Johnathan Harker cemented very strong ties with the British government, even dining with Lord Sailsbury at one point. Fighting monsters is a noble goal, Mr. Harker but how can I be sure that fighting monsters will not allow the British government to bring enough forces to occupy the whole country? Worse, fighting heathen creatures might give the British a reason to legitimize an occupation of Ireland to the British public."

"Oh, for the love of God, I only seek to defend this country sir! Isolating yourselves has made you dangerously vulnerable to their invasion. And if Mr. Churchill thinks he can use P.E.C as a tool to further his own interests then he'll have our gunships and missile tanks to deal with!"

The men looked at each other and muttered among themselves. Quincy felt anxious that their stubbornness would only make the situation worse. Suddenly, Lemass, being somewhat aware of P.E.C's aerial capacities had an idea flash in his head.

"Wait, Mr. Harker, can your air corps fly in supplies to feed our people? Because in case you haven't noticed, our economy is on the verge of collapse and people are on the streets making demands that I'm not sure I can meet."

Thinking on that, Quincy nodded.

"Yes, our airships could be used to ferry in supplies. However, to do this properly, I will need your engineers to set up drop zones for the airships to deploy those supplies. Trust me gentlemen, my men do not have the hostility to your government that the Druids do."

De Valera added warily.

"Mr. Harker, you may send troops but on one condition... you will not build any permanent bases beyond the Anglo-Irish border and when the faery threat is done, your men will leave and pack everything up. Is that understood?"

"Of course, sir."

"Very well then, you've got our permission, Mr. Harker, use it wisely."

"Thank you, sir."

Quincy left the room, almost weak at the knees at the turnaround. He left the Dáil, found a green telephone box and started to dial in a number.

Meanwhile around the Anglo-Irish border was a vast encampment of military equipment. This was no ordinary military base. Arrayed in the base were huge tanks with long gun barrels extending from their turrets while on their backs were huge missile launching devices. A truck with a radar dish was parked by. The circular device on the top of the truck spun around making a beeping noise as other vehicles, mainly half-tracks packed with ammo and supplies, trundled past the radar truck. The men were doing their routine chores while soldiers with fully automatic rifles stood guard at the entrance of the base. On the landing pads at the base were the P.E.C gunships, huge aircraft with propellers arching upwards at the tips of the wings on either side of the aircraft. A small propeller was on the tail fin of the craft and the enormous helicopters were equipped with machine guns, bombs and missiles. Smaller helicopters also equipped with machine guns were perched on the landing pads as were little helicopters known as Gyrocopters. All these aircraft were undergoing their checks by ground crew.

The sun was setting as two P.E.C wings darted overhead. These craft were small silvery coloured twin engine jets bristling with weapons. Some soldiers polishing their equipment they looked up. As he scrubbed his steel helmet, one spoke to his comrade.

"So, are we taking part in Operation Overlord? I hear that was called off again!"

"Yeah, no, we're just here to swat creepy faeries while the regular US and British armies get all the glory of liberating Europe from the Germans! Look on the bright side, I'd rather kill faeries than Germans, faeries are a different species than us."

"Does that make a difference?"

"Yeah, it does."

Some of the troopers chuckled at that. Nearby another group of very different-looking soldiers were being inspected. These men not only had heavier armour, but they had clunky jet packs on their backs. They wore metal helmets on their heads and had their oxygen packs hanging unstrapped from their helmets.

In the central tent, stood a tall, muscular man with greyish white hair and tanned skin. He was dressed in a khaki outfit with sleeves rolled up, while a scar descended down his cheek. He smoked a thick cigar while listening to the radio.

"And now yet another coup has been launched against the German Chancellor. Leading it was a German aristocrat named Dietrich Hellman who claimed he wished to restore the Kaiser Reich!! Alas, he failed and he valiantly refused all offers that the Chancellor made to seduce him. It cost him his life but nevertheless, listen up for more excitement from the BBC!"

The man flicked off the radio and sighed. Hearing the name

"Dietrich" made him feel as if a weight pressed against his chest because he had known Dietrich personally.

His eyes wandered to a photograph depicting himself and a blonde German officer smiling together in a jungle setting. He was startled by the phone ringing beside him. He picked up the receiver and pressed it against his ear.

"Yes? Mr. Harker? This is Commander O'Connell speaking."

"Commander O'Connell, good news, I've finally got permission to deploy troops south of the border!"

"Excellent, Mr. Harker."

"The Fomorians have brought the country to its knees! Head to Connacht!"

"I'm on my way!"

Bastian put the phone down and pulled on his peaked cap on as he ran out of the tent. He passed through the camp and headed towards a jeep. An officer was waiting by the jeep and overseeing the routines of the encampment. Bastian gave his orders.

"Captain Pratinski! Get your choppers in the air! We're heading out!"

"Where to, sir?"

"To Connacht! Let's go!"

Patrinski saluted him.

"Yes sir! Come on boys, let's get a move on!"

Hearing this, other officers rushed to give the signal. The sound of the bugle was enough for the soldiers to gear up for any oncoming battle, suiting up in their helmets, steel body armour and arm themselves with semi-automatic rifles, smgs as well as rocket launchers. Others activated their vehicles and gradually a convoy began to form. The helicopters at the base began to take off and soar into the sky.

As the jeep started to drive, Bastian took the radio.

"Captain Giles of the P.E.C navy, we're heading into Connacht to fight the Fomorians, requesting support, over?"

"Roger that, we have a fleet and carrier on its way from the Atlantic! Just send us the coordinates and we'll be ready to support! Over and out!"

Out in the Atlantic, one of the largest aircraft carriers ever built was on its way across the stormy seas towards the West coast of Ireland. Surrounding it were a variety of ships ranging from battleships to cruisers and to destroyers. Submarines patrolled underneath. All these vessels kept an eye out for any German U-boats that might be intent on attacking the carrier. Flying above the fleet were an array of giant airships, decorated with iron plating and mounted with gun batteries, missiles and machine guns. Two of the airships had three aircraft mounted from underneath their balloon. The carrier blew its horn as it neared the coastline to signal its approach. The fog-horn could be heard all the way as far as Damien's hometown causing both fear and awe in the villagers.

11

Trapped in Elfland

Back in Efland, Brés clasped a spherical crystal ball in his clawed hand as he held it out in front of him. He looked into it as it glowed before him. As it glowed, Brés could see a plane, Phil's plane to be precise. Looking at it, Brés smirked.

"Hmmm… what a quaint contraption this thing is. It's surprising that it was built by simian savages."

A crow flew towards him perched beside him.

"The humans have accepted your declaration of war. Even as I speak, the armies of Men come with weapons far more significant than I have ever seen them wield. The army of Saint Patrick fights our monsters at this time. This venture…"

Brés turned a black look on the crow.

"Continue our attack, the strength of men is their rational mind, it is what has allowed them to create their world of machines! If we can keep them in a permanent state of panic, they won't be able to think straight and there will be more fear!"

"We shall do as you command, sire!"

The crow fluttered off into the dark sky of Elfland. Brés sneered to himself.

"Hmmm, I think it is time to unsettle things for Lugh and his band of merry men."

As he said this, Brés used his magic on the ball and as he did, the skies over the plane began to darken.

Within the plane, Simon and Eric were playing cards and Phil was piloting. Over on the other side of the plane, Damien was looking at the ground below. He could see some trucks, and Irish troops assembling some sort of landing pad. He only hoped that his village wouldn't be under attack. Then he started to hear thunder echoing through the clouds. He looked up, expecting to see a flash of lightning. Instead, he could see the clouds turning pitch black. Horrified by this, he ran to warn the others.

"Mr. Trent? Lord Fitzgerald?"

As Eric heard the thunder, he paused his game.

"My Lord, is it normal to have thunder like that? I don't see any lightning yet."

Simon grinned.

"Eh....probably just the Irish weather, you know, it has a knack for being unpredictable. Ireland has quite a reputation for it."

Damien arrived breathing heavily.

"My Lord Fitzgerald? What time is it?"

Simon took out his watch and checked it.

"Eleven o'clock in the morning. Why?"

"It's getting dark, it's just turned pitch black!"

"Damien, are you drunk? The sky doesn't turn black randomly like that, even during a thunderstorm!"

Damien was angry.

"Do I look drunk to ye, my Lord? I'm not telling a fib! Ye should look outside if you don't believe me!"

Eric stood up and looked out the window. The thunder struck again making Oisín nervous and even causing the plane to rattle. Seeing that the sky was as black as coal, Eric turned back to Simon.

"Unless I'm drunk too, what Damien says is fact. Take a look!"

Simon got up and saw the sky for himself. More thunder sounded and a flash of lightning struck outside, causing Oisín to yelp in fright. Eric patted his head.

"Oisín, calm down, it's alright! This plane should be pretty durable. Good boy."

The plane's lighting had turned on, providing some dim illumination across the plane. Damien tried to keep the panic from his voice.

"Do we even know where we are?"

Eric ran down the corridor, shouting for Phil.

"What in the name of God! Phil! What's happening to us??"

At the cockpit, an airman waiting outside stopped him.

"Sorry sir! The cockpit is out of bounds for non-qualified personnel!"

"Damn it! I need to speak to Phil Rodgers! Something's gone terribly wrong! Everything's become unfamiliar..."

In the cockpit, Phil checked his navigation equipment but as the plane rattled, buttons and lights were flashing all over the controls while his compass was spinning around. Phil was as confused as anyone else on the plane. Up ahead was pitch black so neither he nor Stephen could see ahead. Suddenly a ghoulish face showed up right ahead of them and screamed. The grotesque apparition vanished quickly and suddenly the storms stopped. However, not only was it pitch black but the two pilots had their senses utterly jolted out of them by that apparition. Phil tried to keep his voice steady.

"Lord God! Who needs Egypt or the Congo for their thrills, when we can just have them here in Ireland!"

"I know, I'm not sure I'll sleep easy after that."

Phil rubbed his eyes. He felt as if he was in some sort of nightmare and he wanted to wake up. But he couldn't because he knew this was all too real.

"Stephen, where are we?"

Stephen studied their route from Dublin.

"Well, logically we should have arrived in Connacht by now, that is after all, where the Druid base is. However, the fact that we are in pitch darkness when it is only eleven o'clock tells me that logic has completely gone out the window."

Phil groaned.

"Turn on the spotlights, Stephen, I want to see where we are flying."

The spotlights of the plane switched on and illuminated the area that they were flying over. Looking down, Stephen could see a barren, thorn infested landscape with strange shapes lingering across it. Baffled, he turned to Phil.

"Are we even in Ireland, Mr. Rogers? It doesn't look like Ireland anymore!"

Looking down, Phil agreed.

"I can see where Bram Stoker got his ideas from. We seem to be in some form of Otherworld.

That would explain the sudden alteration in our environment. It's like we just got spirited away into this Otherworld. It is as if we are in some sort of alternative dimension and not a pleasant one at that."

Phil took out his radio and spoke into it in a calm but tense voice.

"Attention all hands…"

Eric, Simon and Damien heard Phil's voice through the intercom.

"This is the captain speaking, hope you are enjoying your voyage! It is my painful duty to inform you that something or someone has spirited us away to some other dimension. We entered this place through a thunderstorm, it is our hope that in flying through one that we will return to some form of normality…"

Damien had the strange feeling of being both alarmed by Phil's news and a wild desire to laugh at how he had framed the message.

Phil continued.

"Nevertheless, in the case of an unexpected interception, I advise you to head to the armoury and equip yourself with weapons. This is Captain Phillip George Rodgers of the Pellucidar Expeditionary air corps giving the orders! Thank you for your attention!"

The intercom message ended but Damien found it difficult not to laugh. Simon looked at him with some concern.

"What's so funny?"

"Captain Rodger's sense of humour. Dad never told me that Sassenachs have a sense of humour."

"Ah yes, he always had a strange form of sarcastic humour but I don't share it. Come on, you heard him, let's head for the armoury!"

The armoury was a relatively small room but it was decorated by racks of firearms ranging from pistols to automatic rifles to Thompson submachine guns. Grenades were stacked in boxes and crates. Other aeronauts in the plane were arming themselves with firearms when Simon, Eric and Damien came in. Eric lifted up a submachine gun.

"It doesn't make much sense, one minute we're flying over Ireland and then the next minute, we're in some otherworld. How in the name of the Lord did that happen?"

Damien had an idea.

"Eh Boss? Lord Fitzgerald? Ever consider that this is Brés' doing? What if he used his magic to whisk us into Elfland?"

Eric frowned.

"Oh yes, oh yes that makes a dreadful amount of sense. Simon, he brought us into Elfland to trap us, didn't he? That means we are in his country and he can do whatever he wants with us, doesn't it?"

Simon nodded thoughtfully.

"Possibly, it makes more sense than us landing randomly in an alternate dimension."

Another question dawned on Damien's mind.

"Wait, if we are, then how do we get out of here? I mean we'll all be dead if we stay too long here!"

Simon had a more practical concern.

"I don't know, but on a more urgent note, do you know how to shoot? Ever fired a gun?"

"Eh...yes, my father taught me how to shoot. He still has his gun hidden in the event of an attack."

Simon laughed, took a scoped rifle off the rack and flung it to Damien. Damien caught the rifle in both hands but it felt very heavy to handle.

"Ye expect me to use this? I'm a country boy from County Mayo, not an Afrikaner from the Transvaal. I could be a terrible shot."

"So, what if you are a country boy? So were the Boers, so were the Yanks in their early days and your own father and his mates when they fought for Collins. Yet you country lads with rifles like that bloodied the British empire in a way that Asia's wealthiest emperors and empresses could only dream about. Trust me, you'll learn to be good with this."

Looking dumbstruck at the rifle, Damien tried to remember what his father had taught him. As he looked at the rifle, he could figure out that it was a bolt action rifle. Looking at the breech, he pulled back the lever to insert the bullet. He settled down to examine it.

Down below, Brés smirked to himself. He could see the plane with all its spotlights flashing in full glory.

"Perfect, I've got the fools, and the Claíomh Solais in one fell swoop."

Perched beside Brés on the wall was a winged reptilian creature that looked like a serpent but had clawed legs to cling onto the wall. It had a long razor-sharp tail. Brés turned to this creature.

"Kill them, then bring me the sword so that I can destroy it."

The creature took off and let out an unearthly screech, summoning many more of its kind. They swarmed towards the plane.

Brés was triumphant.

"Well, they can't escape this time. Lugh is finished."

But the crow was not so sanguine.

"I would not be so optimistic, sire! He is on a machine with humans, a species known for its cunning ways of escaping death."

Seated in the cockpit, Phil looked out to see a swarm of winged reptiles hurtling towards the plane. He murmured to himself.

"Oh dear, it seems that Brés has sent us a welcome party. Nevertheless, we know what to do."

"Attention all hands, this is the Captain speaking, we have incoming bogeys from all directions, open fire. Mr. Trent, now might be a good time to take out your magic sword!"

Phil's crew opened fire using machine gun turrets around the plane. The traces of the bullets lit up the sky around the plane.

As the battle raged outside, Eric took the Claíomh Solais out of the suitcase. Simon and Damien watched him with awe.

"Damien, do you see any sign of a moon out there? If we want the Claíomh Solais to work, we will need a full moon or a full sun!"

Looking out, Damien could indeed see a glowing moon in the distance.

"There is Mr. Trent, but ye might have to go outside if you wish to harness its power and I seriously doubt that the faeries will give ye a chance to do that."

"I know they won't but at the rate we're going, we can only hold out for so long. Come, young man, let's head to the centre of the fuselage, we'll try to unleash its power there. At least there's a turret to protect us at that point!"

The three started to make their way to the centre of the plane with Oisín bounding ahead of them. Suddenly he started to bark furiously and ran further ahead. Eric shouted after him but they could only run after him.

At the back of the plane, the team manning the turret was running out of ammo. Just as they were reloading, the creatures attacked the turret and smashed through the glass. This allowed the creatures to swarm into the turrets at the back, slaughtering the aeronauts manning the guns. Simon, the first to realise the situation, slammed the door to the back of the plane shut just as one of the creatures tried to ram through it. Simon readied his assault rifle and Oisín took up a position beside him, growling menacingly. Simon was surprised.

"Well, hello there, I didn't realize that you had such a thirst for action!"

The door gave way to the pressure of the winged creatures. Simon let out a burst of gunfire, killing the first creature, but another one followed and flew straight at him. He walloped it with the butt of his rifle but that merely angered the creature. It spread its claws to tear him apart but Oisín was there first. He knocked the creature off Simon and dug his paws into it while tearing at it with his teeth. The creature was distracted long enough for Simon to shoot it, causing its head to explode. More of the creatures were crowding through the ruined door when Eric and some more of the crew showed up. The aeronauts opened fire on them while Eric brandished the Claíomh Solais, using it to hack through the creatures. The team were forced to retreat through the corridors, at the cost of two more aeronauts who were slashed to pieces by their otherworldly attackers.

In the cockpit, Phil and Stephen could hear the screams of aeronauts through their radio. Phil transferred control of the plane to Stephen. Grimly, he drew his own gun.

"I'm going back there! I want to see what's going on!"

Phil rushed through the corridor till he met up with Simon, Eric and Damien as they prepared to make a stand.

"What has happened here?" he demanded.

"They got through!! They breached our defences!! We've killed some of them but we're terribly outnumbered!"

Phil turned on Eric.

"Well, Eric! What about that sword of yours? Flesh eating faeries are tearing apart my plane and killing all my crew, so put it to use!"

"Well, I was about to do that, but then Oisín sensed that the men were in trouble so we decided to help them out first. Now if you'll excuse me, this sword needs a moon or a sun to work!"

Grasping the ladder of the central turret, Eric started to climb up to open the hatch.

On the roof of the plane, it was freezing but Eric held up the sword to the moonlight. Seeing him, all the creatures swarmed at Eric like sharks who smelt blood but Eric started to hack through them with the Claíomh Solais, chopping them up like a knife slicing through butter. Then, one of them rammed into Eric knocking him down against the roof. Eric almost dropped the sword but with all his considerable strength he held onto it.

12

Escape from Elfland

From inside, Damien could see the sword dangling down the side of the plane. It was still clenched in Eric's bloodied hand. Damien grabbed hold of the ladder and started to climb. Phil shouted at him.

"Hold on, where do you think you're going my little bunny rabbit?"

"I'm going to help Eric! He's being murdered by this creatures!"

Both Simon and Phil were horrified.

"Damien, I lost a youth your age because of an encounter with a flying reptilian freak! I'm not losing you the same way!"

But Damien paid no heed to Phil's warnings and stubbornly climbed up the ladder and onto the roof. Phil groaned.

"Stupid boy...come on Simon, let's give him cover!"

Outside, the plane seemed to be moving in slow motion, making it possible for Damien to position himself on its roof. He was right behind the winged Fomorian as it raised its claws to slash Eric. Eric raised his eyes to the creature when a bullet smashed through its chest, causing it to fall off him. Eric looked up to see Damien kneeling in front of him with a smoking rifle. Although Eric smiled, they had little time to celebrate as the winged creatures swooped in again trying to whip at both Eric and Damien with their jagged tails.

One winged Fomorian beast managed to grab onto Damien, trying to drag him off the roof of the plane. Damien tried to beat it off using the butt of his rifle but he would probably have been clawed to death had it not been for Phil and Simon who blazed their machine guns from within the turret, shredding the creatures that were attacking both Damien and Eric. Although exhausted and bloodied, Eric lifted up the sword once again to the moon. This time the moon glowed full on it, lighting up all the symbols till the sword glowed brightly. As the sword glowed, Eric pointed it at the swarm, channelling its energy at the monsters and melting most of them. As the surviving creatures flew away in fear, Eric was on the verge of collapsing. Damien grabbed onto him to keep him from falling but Eric was so hefty and heavy that Damien could barely hold on to him. Simon and Phil climbed out onto the roof to help get Eric back inside.

Looking up at this, Brés glared in pure anger. Not only had he failed yet again to kill either Eric or his friends, but he had failed to capture the sword. Turning to his crystal ball, Brés gazed into its depths until the vision of a dragon manifested within it. He growled.

"Kill them! Roast them like meat!"

In the plane, the men were gathered about Eric as he recovered his breath. Suddenly, the roar of a dragon could be heard. This sound caused mixed reactions within the plane. Oisín whimpered, Damien trembled with fear. Phil merely groaned.

"Oh Lord, can they not be a bit more creative than a dragon? I've killed tons of those bastards since World War One! I'm getting too old for this!"

Eric scramble to his feet.

"Let's get out of here!! I don't intend on any of us becoming roast meat!"

"Righto! Let's see if we can find a portal out of Elfland!"

The group scrambled to the cockpit where Stephen was still keeping an eye on the controls. Before Phil could say anything, he heard a beeping noise.

Pausing, he looked and saw that the light beside the fuel symbol was flashing red. Feeling a sense of dread, he looked over and saw one of the propellers sputtering and coming to a halt. Stephen spoke nervously.

"Sir? I think we are running out of fuel, any orders?"

"I know we're out of fuel! The thing is, I don't know what to do but I'm not ready to die today. I didn't survive the War to end all wars so as to die to a horned Elf!"

As Phil sat down and regained manual control of his plane, Oisín started to bark loudly. He seemed determined to attract attention and even stood up on his hind legs pawing at the control panel. Eric called to him.

"Oisín! Stop! Get back down!! Oisín..."

But then Eric halted, as did the others, when they looked out the window. Burning through the darkness was a bright glowing star.

"Look, a star! Look!!"

All of them except Phil gazed in amazement. Phil was too preoccupied with his control panel. "A star? What of it?"

"But it's the first one we've seen in Elfland....what if it's not normally here? What if this is sent by Danu herself to guide us out? I say we should follow it!"

Phil looked about to argue then suddenly pushed his plane to full throttle in the direction of the star. The dragon followed them snarling and glaring at the craft with blood red eyes.

"Eric if this is an illusion, I'll have you shot!"

"Phil, if we don't get out of here, we'll all be dead and you won't have the pleasure of shooting me!"

As they came closer and closer to the star, the whole area around the plane grew bright and the plane began to rattle again.

Suddenly there was a bright blue sky as their plane burst through a sea of clouds and soon the rolling fields of Ireland could be seen below once more.

Phil's voice cut across the cheering of the others.

"Well Eric, I have to hand it to your dog on this one! Gentlemen! Get to the canteen and break out the beer! I think our escape from Elfland merits a little celebration, don't you think?"

But all happy thoughts dissolved as they heard the dragon's rumbling, guttural growl once again. A dread silence filled the cockpit. Simon was the first to speak.

"It seems like we're not the only ones who made it out of Elfland!"

Phil nodded grimly.

"I guess those beers will have to wait until we're firmly on the ground, right lads? Come on,

get your guns out again, I'll need a bit of cover to defend me as I land you all safely!"

13

The men of Saint Patrick

Phil and Stephen struggled to control the drop of the plane as yet another engine sputtered to a halt. The dragon opened its fanged mouth and emitted a flame which set the stern of the plane on fire. Soon the temperature gauge of the plane went right up to red while a light flashed red as a beeping noise emitted from the controls. Phil snapped at Damien.

"Get the fire extinguisher, it's that red tube-like device behind me!"

Damien grabbed the fire extinguisher but hesitated until Eric pointed to the lever.

"Look, it's like a gun. You point it at the fire and pull this lever."

Bursting out of the cockpit, Damien could see that the corridor was now alight and that the metal was starting to melt away. Fighting down a wave of panic, he raised the extinguisher and sprayed foam over the area in front of him, smothering the flames. He continued through the plane spraying more foam until all the flames eventually died out. Behind him, Eric surveyed the remains of the plane. He patted Damien on the shoulder.

"Good work, Damien, you can keep a clear head!"

"Thanks, but the dragon is still out there."

Below them on a rolling hill was a troop of heavily armoured soldiers. They wore green uniforms under their breastplates and shin guards while their heads were protected by Stalhelm helmets. These soldiers had a radio, flak artillery mounted on half-tracks as well as a fluttering banner coloured green with a golden harp.

Their officer wore the same uniform but without any armour. In place of a helmet he wore a peaked cap. Peering through his binoculars he could see the dragon approaching.

"Fomorian dragon incoming! Bring the monster down!"

Immediately, the half-tracks started to fire up at the dragon. However, they didn't manage to hit the dragon's belly. One of the artillery men pointed to Phil's plane.

"Sir! The dragon is attacking a British plane!"

"Doesn't matter, we kill the Fomorian first, then we'll deal with the human machine later! Call interceptors! Tell them to intercept that dragon!"

Back up in the plane, the plane was sputtering to a halt. Over the noise of the plane the men could hear gunfire. Damien turned to Phil in consternation.

"Mr. Rodgers, it appears we're being fired at!"

"Don't worry lad, they're not firing at us, they're aiming for the bloody dragon!"

Outside, the dragon opened its mouth, revealing its razor-sharp teeth as it was about to yank off the tail of the plane. But then, bullets battered against its hide causing it to back away. Swooping in overhead was a squadron of silvery coloured planes that were twin engine propellor craft. Although they were bigger than most fighters of this era, they were surprisingly manoeuvrable and they easily outmaneuvered the dragon as it tried to burn them. On their wings was the insignia of the golden harp on a green background. Observing the great winged beast, the squad leader issued his instructions over the radio.

"Listen up lads! This beast is a big one! I'll use myself as bait to distract it! The rest of ye, target its belly! Over?"

"We understand, Over and out!"

The squad leader let out a burst of ammunition to attract the dragon's attention. The dragon flew after the squad leader in an attempt to take him down but whenever the dragon spewed flame, the plane dodged out of the way, forcing the dragon to turn and follow him. Another fighter swooped up from below and blazed its guns. The bullets struck the belly of the dragon and it went plummeting down to the earth. Damien watched the battle with excited eyes.

"Look, look! Those fighters brought down the dragon!"

"Good for them!" Phil was still preoccupied with his controls.

"Do ye think they are here to rescue us?"

"I wouldn't be so sure of it, Damien, is it normal for Irish aircraft to have a harp on their wings?"

"Not those owned by the free state, no."

Before anyone else could say anything, the sound of the last engine sputtering to a stop could be heard outside.

"Dump as much weight as possible, the lighter the plane, the more chance we have of getting it to glide. If we can do that, we might have a chance of surviving!"

Immediately the others rushed to pick up objects to throw out of the plane. Eric opened the door and felt a gush of heavy wind lash against him. Suddenly he realised that the plane seemed to be gliding to the ground already. Amazed, he turned to the others.

"Gentlemen? It seems that we've got ourselves a wind!"

"A wind? Is it Danu again?"

"It might be, Simon, or it might just be Irish weather but we may not have to dump things in order to glide."

Down below, an officer clasped his binoculars as he could see the plane slowly heading towards the ground. It was as if some sort of force was trying to guide it as safely as possible. Frowning, the officer turned to a corporal.

"Corporal Fionn! Take some soldiers and keep track of that plane! Once it's found, ye will escort the survivors to Lord Donacagh!"

"Yes sir!"

Fionn took several soldiers with him. These men clasped semi-automatic rifles and rocket launchers and they got onto a halftrack which followed the falling plane. As they drove towards it, the plane fell lower and lower to the ground till it struck a field. The force of the plane hitting against the field was so strong that it caused the wings of the plane to be yanked off. When the plane shed its wings, the wings went flying into the tail fins which got knocked off. With both its wings and fins gone, the plane lost momentum and came screeching to a halt. The half-track stopped and the soldiers looked at their leader enquiringly.

"Shall we go in, sir?"

"No! Wait among the bushes and see who comes out! Only fire if they fire first!"

Leaving the half-track, they were accompanied by some wolfhounds as they headed to the bushes and the trees. Observing from the trees they got their rifles ready while two men established a heavier machine gun mounted on a tripod.

The door to the plane opened as Oisín leapt out first, followed by Phil, Eric, Simon and eventually Damien. They all had their weapons with them but none of them were aware that they were being watched. They paused and all sank down on the grass. There were no crops or livestock in the area. Stephen got out of the plane after the others, carrying an ordnance survey map. After all that time in the plane, Damien couldn't help but feel a massive sense of relief to feel soil and grass against his boots, with the knowledge even if he fell he wouldn't be falling to his death. Eric was more worried as he has the uneasy feeling that they were being watched. He looked around to see if there were any signposts visible on the road.

"Gentlemen, landing safely is all well and good, but do we know where we are?"

Simon scratched his head.

"I don't know...we're in Ireland, obviously...but aside from that, we could be anywhere in the country because of what happened."

"Any ideas! There surely must be some town nearby, I can see electric poles along the road."

Phil answered him soothingly.

"Gentlemen! Come on over here, let's take a rest so that we can study the map."

Oisín prowled around as he guarded them. His nostrils twitched as he sensed something. He began to bark. Damien looked up.

"Eh, should we be nervous?"

Phil responded dismissively.

"Don't worry, Damien, Oisín hasn't been on land for days! He's probably chasing a red squirrel. There's a lot of them in Ireland!"

But the unseen wolfhounds began to answer Oisín. Seeing him set off towards the bushes, Eric and Damien scrambled to their feet.

"Hold on! Oisín, come back here!"

Eric rushed after his dog and Damien grabbed his rifle and followed. Simon, Phil and Stephen also reached for their weapons. Just then, soldiers emerged from the bushes. They raised their rifles and pointed them. Undaunted, the gang raised their own weapons and Eric pulled out the Claíomh Solais. They heard the men shouting at them orders in a language that was not English. Phil was puzzled.

"Damien, did your countrymen call the Wehrmacht in?"

But Damien listened closely to what the soldiers were saying and it was a language he knew perfectly.

"Mr. Rogers, that's not German they're speaking!"

Damien raised his hands and shouted in Irish.

"Wait a minute!! We're not your enemies!! We're friends and we're fighting the Fomorians. We come with goodwill!"

The soldiers kept their rifles raised.

"Prove yourself! If ye are lying, ye will be shot!"

Hearing this chilled Damien's heart but he turned to Eric.

"Boss, I think it's time to show them the sword."

"What? What did you say to them?"

"I think these are the Druids! You know, the lads we've been searching for. Didn't Mr. Harker send us out deliberately to find these men and bring the sword to them? Prove to them that we have the sword and they won't shoot!"

Eric slowly raised the sword. Though the clouds blocked the sun's rays, the sword still glowed like gold. The soldiers stopped. The very sight of the enormous glowing sword in the firm hand of a confident red-haired Eric seemed to pacify the encroaching soldiers, causing them to lower their weapons. Corporal Fionn murmured under his breath.

"It cannot be..."

He approached the group, flanked by two soldiers. The men lowered their own weapons as the soldiers approached. Eric spoke to Damien.

"Damien, you understand the Irish language for you have grown up in it."

"What do ye want me to do?"

"Ask them if they are the Men of Saint Patrick and if it was them who killed the dragon back there."

"Boss, you do realise these are the same bunch that tried to kill me and my brother in order to..."

"Damien! Ask them. Remember, as you said, we were sent by

Quincy Harker to negotiate."

Damien took in a breath and spoke to the soldiers in Irish.

"Are ye the men of Saint Patrick? Was it ye who slew the Fomorian dragon?"

The officer responded.

"Yes, we are the Druids, the men of Saint Patrick. We did slay the dragon."

Turning to Eric, the officer added.

"Is this the thief who stole the Claíomh Solais?"

Turning to Eric, Damien said.

"He confirms that his men are of the Society of Saint Patrick. He asks if ye were the one who stole the sword of light?"

Eric groaned.

"They obviously don't know the difference between an archaeologist and a thief."

Eric raised his voice as he continued sternly.

"Damien, tell him that I've been getting visions of Danu herself. That she has guided me to the sword, that I am the reincarnation of Lugh himself and that my current objective is the defeat of Brés and the Fomorians! Tell them that we are here as diplomats as behalf of Quincy Harker of P.E.C."

Damien explained all this to the Druid soldiers. Fionn muttered to his sergeant.

"This man claims to have visions of Ireland herself speaking to him…"

"Although that may seem absurd, sir, that would explain why the plane landed so smoothly without too much damage. The Goddess has been guiding him."

Phil was getting impatient.

"What the hell are they saying, Simon?"

"They're discussing the fact that Eric is getting visions from

Danu..."

"Why are we waiting...we need to..."

"Be quiet, don't do anything stupid. Let Eric and Damien negotiate."

After some conversation, Fionn suddenly switched to English.

"Come with us! We're taking you to Lord Donacagh O'Malley! He will judge if you are trustworthy or not!"

If they were surprised to suddenly hear the Druid officer speak English, they were more than happy not to have to walk so they boarded the halftrack alongside the soldiers. The halftrack trundled onto the road where it joined several other half-tracks which were being led by an armoured car. The squadron that slew the dragon flew over them as it made its way back to the base.

As the convoy moved across the countryside, Phil looked up at the Druid soldiers as they sat like statues. It took him a while to realize that these clean-cut men who in his eyes dressed like German soldiers were in fact the "Druids". They certainly had changed a lot since the reign of Fionn Mac Cumhail. Stephen nudged him.

"What do we do now, sir?"

"We let Mr. Trent, his assistant and Lord Fitzgerald do the talking. Then once contact is established we will inform Mr. Harker."

"And then?"

"An alliance may be struck between the Druids and P.E.C. It would make one of the most powerful armies in the world, the combination of our forces."

The convoy continued its journey.

14

Brought before Donacagh

Eventually, the convoy reached a form of bunker complex that looked to be dug into the side of the hill. Artillery pieces appeared to be sticking out of the bunker and there also seemed to be some sort of array of radio antennas. A radar dish was mounted on the hill. The place left the whole group speechless.

"Is this their base?" Damien asked Simon.

"It is. The Germans built it for them."

"My God! There was a high-tech base in Ireland the whole time, and we didn't know it."

The convoy came to a halt outside the bunker as a light at the side of the entrance flashed red. Soon the light flashed green and the slab that sealed the base slowly started to lift up, allowing the convoy to enter. Inside they found themselves looking around at an advanced complex that had been built underground. The base itself was teeming with personnel who travelled around via trams and electric train systems which also transported cargo. The convoy itself entered the parking lot. There was a vast array of both heavily armoured and heavily armed vehicles that were being tended to by crews of engineers. The halftrack halted and the door opened, allowing everyone to get out. Phil looked around him in amazement.

"Good God! How did people said to be made up of illiterate farmers living on bogs develop a facility such as this? It looks like our own Scraw-Fell! The headquarters of the Pellucidar Expeditionary corps. Wonder how they get their money?"

Eric was also observing his surroundings.

"Funding, I guess? I'm sure Lord Donacagh can answer that,

all this technology looks pretty German yet when I first met them, the Druids said that they had no connection to the Nazis. Interesting."

Simon stepped smartly back as an enormous tank rolled past.

"At least they have harps as their insignia! Mr. Churchill would have heart failure if he saw swastikas on all of these vehicles. He'd think they were working with the Nazis."

Damien was looking at a strange jet shaped device mounted on a tracked chassis. A blocky control panel of some form was mounted on the deck of the machine. The very sight of all this ordnance gave Damien the creeps. Fionn guided them to an elevator. As the elevator went up, Simon turned to Fionn.

"What's with all the German gadgets? Did the Germans build the base?"

"The German designs? Before the Nazis took over Berlin, our society had a link with the German Chancellor Otto Von Bismarck. He sent German engineers secretly to Ireland to help us refit our base with the latest equipment. The Kaisers continued that link. We had a coalition with the German Thule occult society who gave us several blueprints to help us develop our army. They taught us how to manage all of this technology."

"And what happened?"

"When the Nazis took over, Hitler started purging the Thule occult society of members because they had their own army and didn't trust him. His SS saw us as lesser beings so we broke off contact."

"I see."

Eventually, the elevator reached its destination and Fionn guided them to the central office of the base. Damien couldn't stop looking around him at the different statues and paintings that decorated the place. They looked almost as grand as the interior of the Titanic. Guarding the central office were a group of men dressed in uniform. But over their uniform they wore a tartan cape which was kept in place by a brooch which fastened the cape around the neck. A Celtic cross dangled from around their neck and they had sheathed broadswords attached to their belts. Seeing the group arriving, they stood to attention in front of the door. Fionn pointed to Eric.

"We have a man who claims to be a reincarnation of the Pagan God Lugh! He can handle the Claíomh Solais with ease. We wish to speak to Lord Donacagh!"

One of the guards answered him.

"He may enter, Corporal! And one other can come in with him."

Another guard opened the door to allow Eric to enter. Simon, wanting to speak to Donacagh himself, followed Eric. The rest of the group remained outside, closely monitored by the Druid guards.

Inside the office, sitting at his desk was a hefty, well-built man dressed in a dark green uniform. Over that uniform, he wore a long dark cape that was kept fastened by a brooch. His raven hair was closely cropped while the back of his head was totally shaved. He had a black moustache and his eyes were icy blue. He wore a Celtic cross around his neck and behind him was an illustration of Saint Patrick banishing the snakes. The serpentine creatures in the painting were horned, their eyes were blood red and their scales were coal coloured. Such was common among beasts used by the Fomorians. Attached to this man's belt was a sheathed broadsword and he wore boots on his feet.

The guard who preceded Eric and Simon saluted.

"My Lord O'Malley, Corporal Fionn has brought strangers to our base, he rescued them from a Fomorian dragon! One of them has the Claíomh Solais!"

"The Claíomh Solais....let me see him for myself!"

The Druid guards made way for Simon and Eric. Eric held the sword firmly in his hand. Donacagh O'Malley's eyes narrowed.

"Well....well, if it is not Eric Trent? The thief who stole the sword from its resting place under the cliffs of Killala! My men told me all about you, English I presume?"

"Yes, I was born to British citizens but I was raised in France. I am the son of Keith and Elinor Trent."

Donacagh nodded.

"I see. A great many Englishmen have come to this base, Eric....but none of them ever went back to London with a head!"

Simon and Eric looked at each other with pained expressions. Donacagh continued in a mocking voice.

"So, Englishman, what makes you any different?"

"Listen sir! Swallow your contempt towards me and England! Mr. Harker, on behalf of the Pellucidar Expeditionary Corps sent us to negotiate an alliance with you to fight the Fomorians! Lord Brés has devastated Ireland, slaughtered villagers and his creatures have burnt crops and sacrificed children. Do you do nothing about this?"

"Actually Mr. Trent, my army goes out night and day to do battle with Fomorians! But we are quite capable of fighting the Fomorians alone! Mark me, Trent, I have seen Englishmen offer false friendship only to break alliances when it no longer suits them and I do not wish to see Ireland suffer a similarly dark fate! We will not subordinate ourselves to Elfland, to London or to Rome!"

Simon interrupted sternly.

"But we bring the Claíomh Solais as a sign of goodwill! I'm as Irish as you, Lord Donacagh..."

But Donacagh wouldn't have this.

"No!! No!! You do not have the right to claim Irishness! You sir are British!!! And judging by your accent...your ancestors followed King William like slaves!"

"Yet this "Englishman", my Lord, is here to help fight the Fomorians. I wouldn't be if I didn't care about Ireland!"

Donacagh scowled.

"Guards!! Take these Sassenach aliens out of my office!!"

Immediately the guards tried to grab both Eric and Simon, but Eric shrugged them off. A guard brandished his sword only for Eric to parry it with the Claíomh Solais. Immediately the glowing sword caused the men to back off. But they still had their swords drawn. As he saw this, Simon turned to Eric.

"Tell him! Tell him who you really are...tell him what you told me back on the plane! For the sake of all of us! Tell him!"

Eric approached Donacagh pointing the Claíomh Solais at him.

"I am a reincarnation of Lugh! In my past life I led the Tuatha De Danann into battle against King Balor of the Fomorians himself! I have a lineage that traces to the Kings of Agartha, the same species as the Tribe of Danu....and I have been called once again by Ireland herself to defend her and her people from Brés and his hordes! With or without your help that is what I am going to do."

Donacagh looked dumbly at Eric.

"You claim to have talked to Mother Ireland herself? How?"

"In my dreams, my Lord! Ever since I have been in Ireland, these dreams and visions have guided me to the sword of light and have allowed me to find it!"

Donacagh's whole demeanour changed. After a long moment, he spoke in a stern but calmer voice.

"Forgive me for my hostility to you both. I have heard of Ireland hailing people to do noble deeds in her name but I was not expecting such a vision to be had by an Oxford scholar. Follow me if you please."

Eric nodded but he maintained his reserve as he followed Donacagh.

Donacagh led the way out of the office and stopped to talk to Fionn.

"Corporal! Please escort your strangers to the canteen where they can eat. Mr. Trent is coming on a walk with me for I intend to show him something."

He indicated that Eric should follow him.

Fionn beckoned the rest of the group to come with him, not forgetting Oisín.

"How did that go, my Lord?" Damien demanded eagerly.

"Eric told him about being reincarnated and having visions and that calmed everything down..."

"Will we tell Mr. Harker?"

"When we get our hands on a radio we will. His armies must already be here, they will defend your people regardless of what happens."

Eric followed Donacagh and three of his guards. Druid soldiers stood guard before doors throughout the corridors, watching the scenario stoically as Eric and Donacagh walked past them. Eric finally decided to ask the question that had been puzzling him.

"My Lord, may I ask of you, why does a society based around Saint Patrick name its followers "Druids"? Were they not the priests of the old religion?"

Donacagh nodded.

"Our history begins with the dawn of Christianisation in Ireland. When the last of the Fianna, Oisín, returned from Tír na nÓg, he found that his father, his brothers and the old gods were long gone. During this time, he fell off his horse after trying to lift up a boulder. As soon as he touched the ground, he suddenly grew very old. He'd actually been gone for hundreds of years. The Celtic Christian Saint Patrick tended to Oisín in his mission."

"Official legend tells that Oisín died blind after that..."

"Ah yes, his body deteriorated considerably but his mind was as strong as when he first met Niamh on that hunting trip. Oisín learnt that Saint Patrick had banished the Fomorians but he knew that they would return, and without a Fianna to protect her, Ireland would be in a terrible state. That is why he founded us..."

"You mean that..."

"Oisín was the one who founded our society. He forged us to combine both the strength and discipline of the Fianna and the wisdom and scholarship of the Druids. Hence why he called us Druids. We defended Ireland for centuries, even when we lost her lands to English kings, we defended her treasures and her essence from their aggression."

"With German help?"

Donacagh simply nodded again.

"Bismarck was an intelligent leader... such great leadership is a rarity in this mechanical age. Before their current regime, they displayed great nobility, we had no quarrel with the Germans."

"Tell me Lord Donacagh, you said there was another who communicated with Danu in his dreams, who was he?"

"Follow me."

Donacagh led Eric further down the corridor till they came across a large window on the wall. This window overlooked a laboratory. As he peered through the window, Eric couldn't believe his own eyes because in the laboratory was an enormous bronze cauldron with some sort of molten liquid in it. Eric turned to Donacagh.

"Am I really seeing this, it cannot be!"

"It is. For under the wise guidance of W.B. Yeats, we found and dug up the Cauldron of the Dagda before any Empire or thief could lay their hands on it. It is another of the treasures of Ireland brought to her by the Tuatha De Danann."

"Wait, did you say Yeats? You mean Yeats had these visions too?"

"Yes, Yeats was no mere poet. He was a mystic, a member of the golden dawn, and a friend of the Druids. Through his psychic dreams he helped us find this cauldron."

As Eric looked down at the Cauldron, he could see the Druid

scientists tending to the cauldron with the most delicate care as they studied it. Donacagh continued.

"The Cauldron holds many mysteries; legends say that the one who has the cauldron shall prosper. Samples from the Cauldron can heal wounds, even bring back life. But its magic is finite and must be used sparingly. That's why we hide it here. It is not a commodity to be abused for personal gain."

Eric continued to gaze at the cauldron, captivated by what he saw.

Meanwhile in the canteen, Oisín sat down near the bench beside Damien. Fionn was on the opposite bench. As they ate, Fionn chatted to Damien.

"So ye are a country boy, are ye?"

"Yes, Corporal, are ye from the country?"

"No, I guessed ye were from your simple outlook. I'm from Cork, grew up in Cork city. Are your parents still alive?"

Damien began to feel both curious and unsettled.

"What do ye mean? Of course, they're still alive... at least I hope."

"Good, you are lucky. I was raised an orphan, in one of those "Industrial schools" as they called them. Was raised by priests to be appropriately civilized."

"Did they succeed? You joined an organisation that hates "The Church of Rome" after all."

"Our church was the Celtic Church as established by Saint Columba....that "industrial" school didn't succeed in civilizing us or in making us to be good little boys that would just obey their Church. Honestly, be glad ye were raised by your parents, I don't want to remember what happened to me in that...that place. I just know that by the time I was sixteen I was so desperate to get out that I fled. I left that place for good without turning back."

Damien fell silent after that. Judging by the tone which

Fionn used to describe the school, he didn't want to imagine what went on in there. On the opposite side of the table, Phil was talking to Simon.

"When will we inform Mr. Harker that we have established a link with Lord Donacagh?"

"As I said, when we finish our meal, we will get a Druid to escort us to the radio station of the base. Eric seems to have successfully got himself an audience with Lord Donacagh."

"Hmmm....I see."

15

P.E.C arrives in Ireland

In the outskirts of Killala, Seosamh and Donal were walking along the road through a thick ghostly fog that covered the area. Seosamh was beginning to walk well again as his ankle had recovered from his accident at the dig. Life had gotten harder for the O'Laoghaires since Brés declared his war on humanity. Soldiers now occupied the town to defend it from attacks. However, they also enforced curfews in the evening. People weren't allowed to go too far from the town unless under armed escort. Donal had taken out his pistol that he still had since the Irish Civil war, it was firmly in his pocket. As they walked, Seosamh was grumbling.

"Do ye think the Lockdown is going to end? How many more weeks do we have to queue for bread? It's like what they say about the Soviet Union, yet we call ourselves a Free State?"

Donal sighed.

"Well, I'm not going to lie to ye about this, Seosamh, I doubt it's going to change much till this war ends...and I can't tell ye how or when that will happen. The faeries are an unpredictable lot altogether."

"Do ye think Damien will return?"

"Ye all miss him, don't ye? But the Lord knows where he is! He hasn't even got in touch with us, and that makes me fear the worst Seosamh."

"Dad, it was my idea to look for that sword...I feel like I helped start this mess..."

"Ah don't be like that, Seosamh. If it weren't the Sword of Light, I'm sure they would have found another reason to go to war with us!"

Seosamh still sighed sadly. He wondered how differently things would have gone if he had kept his mouth shut that night and not encouraged Damien to go seeking the Claíomh Solais. He was jolted out of these reflections by a rumbling noise. It first sounded like a roar and then like many engines at once. Seosamh stopped in his tracks.

"Dad, do ye hear that?"

Donal listened as the rumbling noises got louder. The two of them gaped in disbelief as clattering out of the fog emerged a giant tank with a long gun barrel and a chunky missile launcher on its back. The P.E.C insignia was on its turret. Donal and Seosamh jumped onto the grass at the side of the road so as to not get trampled. As the tank clattered past them, they could see soldiers perched on its back. These soldiers were clad in heavy armour such as breastplates, shin guards and semi-circle steel helmets. This gear was camouflaged and they clasped semi-automatic rifles and submachine guns. Soon several other tanks emerged from the fog. Seosamh was terrified.

"Dad? Look! I didn't realize our army had tanks like that!"

"They don't! Seosamh, run to your mother! I'll warn Colonel Maloney, he's the head of the garrison at our village!"

Seosamh ran as fast as he could. Above him he could hear the sound of propellers hidden by the clouds. He could hear a disembodied voice of a radio command coming from one of the vehicles.

"Alright gentleman, we're approaching a local settlement, stay at the ready."

Coupled with the sight of all these vehicles bristling with heavy weapons, Seosamh felt completely spooked out.

Back at the town, a tense atmosphere reigned. The bells of the church rang while soldiers were placing sandbags around the village and mounting big machine guns onto tripods. Artillery was being positioned around the village, maneuvered into position by trucks and armoured cars. A radio station was located near the town. In the meantime, townsfolk still went around about their business. Sarah was waiting with the twins in a queue behind a long line of other people. They waited as the soldiers and guards delivered them supplies of bread. Suddenly Sarah became aware of Seosamh's voice yelling.

Turning around, she saw Seosamh running towards her.

"Mam! You won't believe this! There's a huge batch of soldiers coming from the North... they've got big tanks!! They'll be coming here!!"

"Seosamh, calm down...where's your Daddy?"

"He's gone to warn the Colonel about the "machine army". It's from the North, isn't that where all the Unionists reside..."

Sarah rolled her eyes.

"So even with the faeries running amok, we still get dragged into politics. Personally I think we'll need all the help we can get."

At the church, a smartly uniformed General was overseeing the defence of the town. The parish priest was standing with him, observing the installations,

"Ye are doing well, General Maloney. Ever since the deployment of your troops, not a single villager has been slain. The Lord is aiding us in this time of peril."

"I know, Father Fitzpatrick, but the defence of as many towns as possible puts immense strain on our resources. Already, many good men have died to the most horrific beasts. At least when we fought the British, we fought an enemy we knew."

"Well, the death toll would be worse if ye stood idly by. Evil is at its strongest when good men do nothing.... have courage, General, help will surely come even if it is from the most unlikely of places."

"I can only hope so Father, I don't know how long our State can resist on its own."

Their discussion was interrupted by someone shouting. The General turned to see Donal rushing towards him. Maloney's sombreness turned to anger.

"Well, what is it now O'Laoghaire! You are always getting involved in our plans as if you are the most important person in the village... come on, speak!"

An exhausted Donal saluted him.

"General? Sir! I need to warn ye, an army of tanks and mechanized soldiers is coming to the town! It is an army of men more powerful than anything I've seen before. It comes from the North of Ireland!"

The general, not having been informed about Quincy's agreement in the Dáil raised his eyebrows.

"The North? O'Laoghaire what do you mean by the North? Sending an army into Ireland without warning? No, not even Churchill would violate our neutrality like that!"

"General, ye've got to believe me!"

But then the General heard the clattering and the sound of engines and turned to see the convoy approaching. The Irish soldiers loaded every weapon they had so that they could be at the ready in case of an attack. The oncoming tanks drew to a halt in a line. Behind the tanks came self-propelled artillery, armoured cars mounted with missiles on their turrets and armoured half-tracks packed with heavily armed and heavily armoured infantry. There was even a truck with a radar dish that was constantly spinning while emitting a beeping noise. Behind that truck were all the supply vehicles and even a long truck equipped with gyro copters. Before this array of machinery, the Irish soldiers did not move an inch. Peering through his binoculars, an officer watched a jeep approaching. Sticking out of the window of the jeep was a white flag. Seeing this, the officer ran back to the General.

"Sir, they're waving a white flag, it seems that they mean no harm, they might be willing to negotiate!"

"Keep the troops on alert! For all we know this could be a Trojan horse trick."

Meanwhile at the village centre, Donal reunited with his family. As they embraced, Sarah wept with relief.

"Donal? What in God's name is happening?"

"Sarah, I've warned the Colonel about the oncoming army..."

One of the twins, Aidan tugged at his arm.

"Hey, Dad, look up there! Isn't it big?"

Donal heard the buzzing noise of propellers above him and noticed that other villagers were panicking. Looking up, Donal saw a giant P.E.C gunship bristling with weapons above. The soldiers in the town raised their rifles up to aim at it. It didn't fire a single weapon but the very sight of such a behemoth spread panic among the people below. Out of terror, a cart horse reared as its master tried to calm it down. The people of this simple town had never seen technology like this before.

The General kept calm as the jeep slowly approached the town. Riflemen guarding the town had their eyes like hawks upon the jeep as they focused their rifles on it, tracking its movements thoroughly. As the jeep drove towards the central fountain, many of the children tried to approach it because such a vehicle was not a sight they saw every day. However, they were kept away from the jeep by both their parents and the guards. They were even more in awe when they saw the gunship above. The jeep stopped. The soldiers kept their guns at the ready. The door opened as tall, gaunt man stepped out with a cigarette in his mouth. He was followed by his officers who kept their hands within view. The stranger glared around him.

"Well so much for the friendly hospitality of the Irish! Who's in charge?"

General Maloney descended the steps of the church.

"I am, and Irish hospitality is not friendly when you come into a town with tanks, guns or whatever that contraption is up above us! What's your business here?"

"My name is Francis Bastian O'Connell of the Pellucidar Expeditionary Corps! I thought Mr. Harker got me permission from the Dáil to come here, did the Taoiseach not inform you?"

The General didn't answer. He had not been told about the fact that P.E.C was coming here.

Bastian laughed sarcastically as he ground out his cigarette.

"Right. I'll take that as a no. Poor communication on the government's part."

Bastian turned to the crowd gathered behind them.

"Ladies and Gentlemen!!! I've come to invade Elfland itself and defeat the Fomorians!!! You may not want my help being the proud people you are but by God, you will need it!"

Curious and concerned, the General finally found his voice.

"What do you want in return for fighting the Fomorians for us?"

Bastian looked at him steadily.

"All I wish for is for you to not attack my men and in return we will set up a base camp in the proximity of the village."

Donal stepped forward.

"Will ye help us fight the Fomorians when they attack our town?"

"Yes! We will, and when they are dealt with, we will leave! How does that feel?"

That made the people feel more comfortable and the riflemen lowered their rifles. The General visibly relaxed.

"Very well, you may set up camp."

That night, Donal watched as the P.E.C army set up camp. Notably, their electric spotlights helped to brighten the otherwise pitch-black countryside. But their vehicles were loud enough to be heard from the town. He was still suspicious, for he wanted to see them in action first before he could truly trust them.

◆ ◆ ◆

Back in Elfland, Brés was sitting upon his throne when a crow once again perched itself in front of him.

"I fear our attacks upon men have had the opposite effects to what we hoped for, sire! They have brought a huge army from the Albion controlled North. This army has some of the most powerful machinery forged by men. In their anger and their fear towards us, they have positioned their soldiers everywhere."

"Enough! I have heard enough of this discouragement! Where is Lugh? I am tired of him outwitting us and escaping us!"

The crow preened himself before responding.

"Lugh and his friends are in the company of the Druids, to forge an alliance between the Druids and Albion. Within the Druid stronghold is the Cauldron of the Dadga. My Lord, if we could bring that cauldron to Elfland, we could resurrect Balor and his army. Such an army almost conquered Ireland successfully before Lugh slew Balor. No mortal weapon can stop the beasts of Balor!"

Brés got up from his throne and clenched his fists. He went up to the walls of his fortress and clasped a Horn. Seizing the horn, he blew into it, letting out a haunting and loud noise across Elf Land.

Suddenly all sorts of monstrosities emerged from the hills and mountains of Elf land. This included grunts, the Fomorians themselves, witches and warlocks, trolls, horned dragons, goblins, black hounds and many more monstrosities. Raising his voice, Brés addressed the hoard.

"Creatures of the night! Kings and Queens of the dark! There was a time when we ruled Ireland, when we held every beast and bird in fear of our wrath! That was before the Tribe of Danu came! That was before mortal men came with their iron…"

The creatures howled and barked in response.

"Take back Ireland! Make it the feared and haunted island it once was!! Leave no man, woman or child standing so that Ireland may become Elfland once more!!"

The creatures roared and screamed as they proceeded through the different portals that led into Ireland. Brés watched them go then decided to observe the scene from his crystal ball. He muttered to himself.

"We will get back the Cauldron....once the humans are appropriately distracted."

16

Attack on the Druids

That night, Eric and the others were sleeping in surprisingly comfortable beds with a room to themselves. As Eric slept, he suddenly felt a presence near his bed. He opened his eyes as he heard the name "Lugh". He sat up, seeing Danu herself by his bedside. Eric was alarmed. "Danu? Eire? What have you to tell me my Lady?"

"I have ill news for you that you must tell the Druids! Brés comes with an army, he seeks the Cauldron of Dagda."

Eric widened his eyes in shock.

"What? What for?"

"He intends to resurrect Balor, for Balor can summon an army that no mortal weapons can pierce. If he succeeds this land will become his!"

"When will this happen?"

"He comes now, Lugh. Warn the druids!"

Eric woke gasping. He scrambled out of bed and quickly got dressed. Oisín who had been sleeping beside Eric's bed raised his head and looked inquiringly while Eric checked his watch.

"I know, Oisín, it's the early hours of the morning but this is urgent!"

He patted Oisín on the head.

"Come on, let's go."

Eric grabbed the Claíomh Solais and left the room, unaware that Damien had woken up as well.

Concerned at seeing Eric leave with the sword, he jumped up

and dressed himself in a Druid uniform, slinging his rifle over his shoulder so that he would appear less conspicuous in the base. He ran after Eric until he caught up with him near Donacagh's office.

"What's happening, Mr. Trent? Why are ye in a hurry?"

"No time, Damien, Danu has warned me of an incoming Fomorian horde. Lord Donacagh must be informed!"

Two guards stood guard at the door. Eric addressed them sternly.

"Warn your master!! Lord Brés of the Fomorians comes with an army. He comes for the cauldron!"

"Who? Who told you this?"

"Danu, Danu told me in a vision! If we tarry, it might be too late!"

Upon hearing the name "Danu", the Druid guard shifted from sceptical to alarmed as he knocked on the door.

In answer to Donacagh's response, the guard rushed in.

"Mr. Trent has had another vision of Danu. Brés' army is coming for the Cauldron!"

"What? Sound the alert!! Everyone must be awake!!"

A great commotion ensued as everyone in the base woke up to the sound of alarms. Everyone hurried to arm themselves. However, before heading out to fight, the Druids all headed to their church. Damien grabbed Simon.

"My Lord? Where do ye think they are going?"

"To pray! They're off to pray for the upcoming battle ahead!"

Curious, Phil, Simon and Damien entered the church themselves.

In the church, the Druid soldiers held their helmets and caps in their hands as a green robed priest dressed similarly to Saint Patrick conducted a service spoken in the Irish language. Once the ceremony was done, Donacagh headed towards the altar. Over his uniform, he wore a tartan cape with his sword sheathed at his side. Druid musicians started to play drums.

Damien looked around, smiling.

"What's happening now, they don't do Mass like this in my hometown."

"I believe he's going to give them a speech, they are saluting his presence with their drums."

Damien couldn't help but feel in awe as he saw Donacagh raised his clenched fist which caused the band to stop playing. There was a moment's silence before Donacagh spoke.

"Noble brothers!! For centuries, we have defended the Celtic culture from alien threats of all forms! Now the hour of our greatest war is at hand! Brés comes to our sacred island with greed and overbearing pride in his heart! Will we allow this?"

"No!! No!!"

"Will we spill Fomorian blood and make it clear that Ireland is not for the taking? After having spent so many centuries of occupation by foreign powers, first the Norse, then the Normans and then England shall we allow the Fomorians to have a piece of our island or shall we fight them!!"

"Yes!!!"

The chapel became loud with cheering.

"For God!! For Saint Patrick and for the Golden Harp…"

Donacagh raised his sword.

"EIREANN GO BREA!!!"

The cheering grew louder and the drums rattled. Damien could even hear pipes starting to play. Phil grinned.

"Well, I have to hand it to the Irish!! They do know how to make a good show."

The pipes and the drums were still playing as the men marched to man the various bunkers that were around the base. Damien looked at the others.

"What do we do now?"

Before anyone could respond, Lord Donacagh approached them.

"So, you are here on behalf of Quincy Harker, the son of Johnathan Harker and leader of the Pellucidar Expeditionary Corps?"

"Yes sir!"

"I've got word from our scouts that his army has arrived in Ireland! They say they are led by an American named Bastian."

Hearing that, Phil punched the air with his fist.

"Yes!"

Donacagh looked at him oddly.

"Then call him, tell him that we are under attack. The Cauldron must not fall into enemy hands and if ever it does, it must be retrieved! You can use my radio."

"Of course, my Lord."

Back at Killala, a formidable P.E.C encampment had been established. Among the array of tents, the soldiers were doing their usual morning routines as spotlights and electric lamps lit the area. The fleet of helicopters were being maintained and refuelled by engineers while all the vehicles were parked in position. At the centre of the camp was the radar truck. A ladder provided access at the back of the truck while the radar dish spun constantly, emitting a beeping noise. There were radio antennas connected to the truck as well. Soldiers stood watch for any intruders.

Inside the radar truck was a buzz of activity as operators observed the map, the radar screen or used the telephone. Bastian was there with his officers when he heard the noise of spinning blades outside. He climbed down the metal ladder of the truck and stood in the wet Irish grass, looking up to see a small helicopter touchdown on a spare landing pad. A pilot wearing a metal helmet and oxygen mask came out of the helicopter. After taking off his oxygen mask, he proceeded to open up the door of the helicopter. Out of the helicopter came Quincy Harker. Bastian saluted him as he approached asking.

"Mr. Harker! Sir! The army has been assembled and we are ready to invade Elfland. Captain Giles Price is out in the Atlantic with a fleet....is there anything else we can do?"

"I need a jeep to head to the Defence Force Colonel here, I learnt that there was some commotion here when you arrived at Killala."

"They didn't seem informed of our permission to come here, sir."

"I know and I need to clarify that. Where is he?"

"He's in the town, Mr. Harker."

Bastian watched as Quincy got into a jeep and drove off to the town. At that moment, Captain Pratinski came out of the truck, calling his name.

Bastian turned to acknowledge his captain's salute.

"Talk to me Captain?"

"It's the Druids, they need support. Phil Rodgers was the one who alerted me!"

"Good, that will help our potential alliance, get me a gunship and assemble the fleet!"

"Yes sir!"

Back at their stronghold, the Druids were installed in the various bunkers that guarded their base, manning their machine guns, artillery and even flame throwers. Train and tram networks transported personnel and munitions between the different bunkers. Damien and Eric waited at the central bunker complex. As Damien positioned himself in the bunker overseeing the land around, Fionn was there manning a machine gun. He grinned cheerfully at Damien.

"You know how to use your rifle, Mayo Man? And you seem to be in uniform?"

"I know I am uniformed yet I'm not one of you but I learnt to use this rifle in Elfland. We got trapped there for a while! The fact that it is scoped and precise made its handling easy."

"Well at this rate we don't care, we're glad to have anyone we get our hands on in this fight!"

Within the hall that was behind the entrance, Druid soldiers positioned themselves behind sandbags. Supporting them were some tanks and armoured cars. They had deployed machine guns and artillery guns. A brutally tense atmosphere developed as everyone had their fingers on the triggers. Donacagh oversaw the whole position as he looked into the still darkened sky. Looking at his watch, he could figure out that it was one o'clock in the morning. For now, all the Druids could see was pitch black darkness. There was nothing more to do but wait.

Suddenly a scream could be heard across the land, a scream that unsettled even Donacagh and his guards. Following the scream, a thick white fog descended across the countryside around the base. As the fog settled, shadowy figures could be seen and the men could hear chanting and roaring coming from the fog. Damien looked at Eric.

"Is that not how the Tuatha De Danann arrived in Ireland?"

"They arrived in cloud ships, not fog. The Fomorians use the fog to transport their number."

As the fog retreated, Brés' army revealed itself. Although the sheer variety of monsters looked to be from nightmares, the Druids didn't appear intimidated. Once the monsters appeared, the battle began. Warlocks used their spells to launch fireballs at the bunkers, but the fireballs only bounced off the rock-hard walls of the bunker. Huge horned beasts tried to slam against the gate of the Druid's base. Druid soldiers fired back at the horde of monsters, killing many of them. Fomorian archers fired arrows, causing the Druids to retreat back from the windows. Some of the arrows embedded themselves against the bunker only to fall off to the ground below.

But just then, a Druid got slammed against the wall with an arrow as big as a ballista bolt sticking out of him. A fireball struck against the bunker. Damien could see warlocks in the distance. Fionn called to Damien.

"You've a scoped rifle, do ye think ye can take out those freaks?"

"I'll see."

Damien focused his rifle on a warlock and peered through his scope. He could see the warlock clearly. He fired at the warlock. The rifle let out a shattering noise and its bullet was armour piercing. It also had a powerful recoil, but Damien finished the warlock after a few shots. Behind him, Donacagh conferred with an officer.

"How is the battle going?"

"The bunkers are holding out, My Lord! Shall we send out tanks and interceptors?"

"No need! This is an awfully weak army for a King trying to seek the Cauldron! I was expecting a more formidable horde! No one is to leave this fortress till the battle ends, it is easy to hide armies in these glens!"

The battle continued and dragged into a stalemate because the bunkers were solid. The Druid soldiers blazed their artillery and machine guns against the horde, slaying many monsters. The train system helped to keep the bunkers constantly supplied with fresh munitions. Studying the battle, Eric observed to Damien.

"So much for the horror of the Fomorians, young man......they fall to an army not using its full strength!"

"That's easy to say when we're safely behind a bunker."

"Ah Damien, don't worry, I'm sure your home is safe."

All of a sudden, the horde started to be battered and torn apart by missiles and gunfire from above which caused the creatures to panic. Curious, Eric looked up to see a P.E.C gunship shining its spotlights at the creatures, followed by more of its type, all of which were escorting an armoured airship. All of these aircraft opened fire on the Fomorians below which forced them to retreat. Peering up at these extraordinary machines, Damien wasn't quite sure what he was looking at..

"Is that a helicopter, Mr. Trent?"

"Yes, it's a gunship, essentially what happens when you combine the hovering capabilities of a helicopter and the firepower of a warship!"

"Lord God....I thought helicopters were only in their infancy, I never thought I'd see one for myself. It's huge."

"Indeed, that is the Pellucidar Expeditionary Corps for you, young man."

Damien could hear the horn of a Fomorian blowing the retreat. Although the sight of the Fomorians fleeing caused some Druids to cheer, Donacagh remained concerned. He muttered to his officer.

"That was too easy for my liking..."

"Maybe he's testing our defences, My Lord."

"Indeed, we should maintain our guard!"

Another officer approached Donacagh.

"Sir, the gunship that has just driven off the Fomorians requests permission to land in our aerodrome!"

"Open the aerodrome, let us meet these Americans..."

"Yes, sir!"

Later, the underground aerodrome of the Druids opened itself by pushing back a slab of artificial grass that hid it from the rest of the world. A landing pad elevated itself up onto the surface allowing the gunship to land on a helipad. Once the gunship's blades stopped spinning, the gunship was lowered down underground into the hangar and the top closed over once more. In the hanger, Phil, Eric, Damien and Simon waited alongside Lord

Donacagh and his guards and soldiers. The door on the side of the gunship opened and a ladder was lowered down. Out of the gunship came Bastian himself followed by some officers. Although the environment felt formal at first with Bastian and Donacagh saluting each other, all sense of formality disappeared when Bastian noticed Phil and Simon.

"Lord Simon Fitzgerald? Phillip George Rodgers? Well, if it is not my old friends!"

"Francis Bastian O'Connell....our old commander!!"

All three men laughed as they embraced each other. The Druids stood stoically while this reunion took place. Damien whispered to Eric.

"Are they mates?"

"Oh of course they are, they have been friends since I was a boy. It is they that saved me from being sacrificed by monsters in Hollow Earth."

"So, one advantage of this mission is bringing the lads together again, aye?"

"I guess so."

Bastian was speaking to Simon.

"Simon, my long suffering second in command who patiently handled my temper! How has life been since you retired in 1938?"

"Relatively uneventful, I reclaimed my estate near Belfast and then, well, my retirement got interrupted by the outbreak of the Second World War, and now the Fomorians."

Phil chuckled.

"Indeed, if our little trip in Elfland told us anything it's that we're getting too old for monster fighting."

"Yes, I know we're all getting too old for this but it's good to see you two again. Quincy Harker has arrived in Killala where our base has been set up. He's currently going to speak with Colonel Maloney on how to coordinate a defence of the countryside!"

Bastian turned to Eric and gasped.

"Eric Trent! Eric if there is one thing you inherited from your mother is that time is your best friend. Time is always kind to those of Tilean blood. You've grown into a living Greek God!"

"Alas, when you are the last of your race that is more a curse than a blessing. I'm going to outlive you all if I survive this mission. I shall never have a wife or child, for your species is too short lived..."

"Yes, longevity must hurt when you are still youthful but still your old man would be proud if he saw you now. You've turned from a helpless child hiding behind his mother from giant spiders into the man who will eventually slay Brés."

Bastian could see the Claíomh Solais in Eric's hand. However, he made no move to touch it. Damien tried to smile politely but he felt his body shiver as he felt small in the presence of Bastian. Turning to Damien, Bastian's mood changed slightly.

"And what do we have here? You look like one of the townsmen at Killala....scrawny and neglected but with the potential for greatness. What is your name?"

"I'm Damien, Damien O'Laoghaire sir, I helped Eric find the Claíomh Solais. He took me to the museum and I've helped him on this journey. Even shot a winged Fomorian trying to kill him when we were trapped in Elfland...I..."

Damien felt like he was spluttering but Bastian patted him on the shoulder.

"I see, well, Damien, my boy it is always handy to have a man of your type around when you need him. Folks of your origin helped build my country, even fighting to win our civil war. Keep that in mind, some of our greatest generals and statesmen were descended from hungry peasants like yourself."

Damien asked nervously.

"You know you are right about Killala, sir, I am from there. Has my hometown been attacked?"

"Damien my boy, I assure you that we have a base in that area ready to respond to any attack...."

This reassuring speech was rudely interrupted.

"Commander O'Connell!! Commander O'Connell!!"

Bastian turned to see an Aeronaut frantically running down the steps of the gunship's ladder.

"What is it?"

"Sir, we got news from Captain Pratinski! Our radar has detected large numbers of Fomorian troop movements headed for Killala. The attack on this base must have been a diversion!"

Hearing that, Damien turned pale. He muttered under his breath.

"Oh no..."

Oisín growled in sympathy. Donacagh began to issue orders.

"Unsurprising! It is as I feared!! Send out our army!! We can deal Brés a major blow!! Brothers, let us prepare for battle!!"

Donacagh turned to Bastian.

"Bastian go on ahead and muster your men!! We head for Killala and for war!!"

Immediately, the Druids rushed for their vehicles while the friends boarded the gunship. Damien's horror turned to awe as he climbed inside the gunship because it was the most technologically advanced machine he had ever been in. He could hear the pilots making their checks as he buckled himself in on a seat. He looked out the window as the platform elevated them back up to the surface. Bastian took a seat beside him.

"Well, O'Laoghaire, how's your experience with flying?"

"Eh....I flew in Phil's plane I guess so I've had some experience."

Phil grinned at him.

"Don't worry, if worse comes to worst, there is a toilet in the rear!"

Oisín leapt up beside Eric as the gunship's propellers began to turn and it took off. Meanwhile, the Druid army prepared for war. A fleet of helicopters was elevated onto the surface so that they could take off. These twin propelled helicopters were bristling with weapons such as machine guns and missiles.

Back in the aerodrome, an armoured zeppelin was being prepared. Its engines were on wings that extended from either side at the back of the airship. Both missile launchers and devices containing racks of bombs were mounted on the wings while machine guns were mounted all around the airship. Underneath the airship's stern was of course a vast cockpit that contained the bridge. Such a device was one of the last of its kind, assembled by the Thule occult society for war against evil forces. Most of its type had been destroyed by the society to prevent them from being used by the Nazis. It was in this airship that Donacagh entered. As the crew began the flight checks, Donacagh gave orders to one of his guards.

"Take some soldiers and guard the cauldron! If any Fomorian comes, even if it is Brés himself, defend the Cauldron at all costs! Understood?"

"Yes, my Lord!"

"Warn me if it falls into enemy hands!"

"I will my Lord!"

The guard jumped off and headed back into the base. A crewman closed the door to the tower as the ground crew cleared the area. All ramps retreated from the area as the propellers of the airship started to spin.

The airship was elevated on its landing pad to the surface to take off. As it did so, Donacagh looked down from the cockpit of the airship as he saw his army deploy. Down on ground was a fleet of tanks, armoured cars, armoured half-tracks and even self-propelled rocket artillery. Motorcycle side cars drove alongside the vehicles while heavily armoured soldiers waited inside the half-tracks. Up on the airship's decks, Druid soldiers wearing oxygen masks manned heavy machine guns.

17

The battle for Killala

In Killala, the sky grew dark grey as clouds blocked off the sun. A ghostly fog was pouring over the countryside. Wind blew against the town, causing the Irish Tricolour to flap wildly while a large flock of crows came flying overhead, croaking loudly. Observing this, the priest spoke nervously to General Maloney.

"It's a bad sign, General...That's a lot more crows than usual."

"Well Father, you don't need to be some sort of symbologist to figure out what that means..."

The General turned to an officer and shouted.

"Sound the alert! The town is under attack!"

The officer took out a bugle and started to blow into it. The soldiers rushed to man their defences and prime their weapons. Donal stood gazing out of the window as Sarah came to stand behind him.

"Donal? What is going on out there?"

"We're under attack by the Fomorians! That bugle is the alarm for the army. Keep the children inside!"

"What are ye going to do?"

"I'm going to find my old guns. Still have a few from the last war."

Donal rushed downstairs and opened the cupboard. Slowly, he pulled out his old revolver. For a while he looked at it, for though he was much older and far less youthful, the sight of the revolver combined with the sound of the bugle made him think of the old days when he was young and fighting for his country's freedom.

Back outside, General Maloney stormed to the radio station.

"We fight till every last drop of ammunition has been spent! There will be no running back to Cork or to Dublin!"

"Yes sir!"

Quincy approached him.

"General....I warn you; this Fomorian army is far too big for your forces to handle on our own, I'd advise not going on the offensive!"

"Mr. Harker! This force is a defence force so we are staying on the defensive! Don't tell us what to do, we know what we are doing!"

"My apologies, General, I'm merely giving advice…"

"Oh, and about that army that showed up on our doorstep yesterday afternoon! Would it mind giving us a hand if these Fomorians are so terrifyingly mighty?"

"Rest assured General, P.E.C forces are on the way, and our air force is taking off in the Atlantic!"

In the stormy Atlantic, on the P.E.C carrier, fire spewed from the engines of a giant assault jet. The craft was yellow and mounted with turrets all around. Missile launchers were mounted on its wings. Its crew wore armoured suits with oxygen tanks. The all-clear had just been given. The craft let out a booming noise as it darted across the carrier's runway before shooting up into the air. Smaller twin engine fighter jets followed. They flew over a fleet of ships, several of which had either the Union Jack or the Stars and Stripes fluttering alongside the P.E.C insignia. Supporting them were P.E C's armoured airships which followed behind at a slower pace. This included the airship aircraft carriers who launched their own jets.

Back at the town, a horn echoed through the fog, followed by the howling of orders. For a while, there was silence among the soldiers who tensely waited among their barricades. But then the sound of loosened longbows was followed by the sky becoming even darker with a hail of arrows. Anyone in the open rushed for cover while the soldiers scrambled for their barricades. Nonetheless, some were impaled with the large arrows. General Maloney paled with shock.

"Sweet Christ, this is worse than in the Westerns! I'd rather have the usual Irish rain."

His attempt to stay light-hearted was short-lived. The fog receded into the distance revealing a horde of both grunts and Fomorians. The grunts howled and snarled as they waved their spears. The Fomorians on the other hand waited behind the grunts. Fomorian musicians played their own pipes while crows fluttered around them croaking. Other Fomorians banged huge drums.

Looking down on the fortified town, a Fomorian chieftain said.

"Send in the grunts first. Let them waste their metal on the grunts. Have our troops follow behind, they will inflict the real damage against the Irishmen!"

Hearing this, a Fomorian warrior blew a horn shaped like a boar tusk and then turned to the grunts. He cracked his whip against the grass causing the grunts to howl and start charging at the town while waving spears and clubs. Behind them, the Fomorians clasping their shields and spears and to the sound of drums marched in disciplined lines. As the Fomorians came closer and closer to the town, Quincy uttered,

"They march! Oh, General, they march as did when they advanced on Camelot!"

"Camelot?? Well then, it's time to give them a reminder that this is the 20th century! Start giving them hell lads!"

And with that, the artillery opened fire. As they marched, the Fomorians could hear the thundering noise of cannons. Then their formations started to be ripped to shreds by shrapnel. When a shell hit, it created a blast that just tore through their shields. The grunts were whipped into charging at the town's fortifications only to be mowed down by machine guns and rifles of the army. Seeing their fellow grunts being mowed like wheat for the harvest, the grunts started to panic and they turned and fled from the town. Their task master tried to get them to fight by whipping them but they fled...only for the Fomorians to start stabbing them. Feeling a sneaking sympathy for the grunts, some of the riflemen targeted the Fomorians in particular, allowing some grunts to escape.

The sheer amount of ordnance being used against the Fomorians caused a total breakdown in their formation. Some charged on but the Irish wasted no time in gunning down as many as they could. Finally, a horn was blown in retreat. Rather than a disciplined retreat, there was a total rout as the Fomorians went back up the hill. Looking at the number of corpses strewn across the battlefield, a soldier asked his comrade. "Is that it?"

"Oh no, Patrick, I believe that is only the first wave."

"The first wave...oh, by the Virgin Mary, Mother of Christ, look up there!"

The soldier looked up with dread as he saw a Fomorian witch with flowing white hair raise her clawed hands in the distance. The riflemen tried shooting at her but as they did, their barbed wire came alive. It started to slither up the sandbags and wrap around their uniformed bodies. The soldiers started to panic and scream in pain as the wire dug into their flesh, coiling around them like a snake before flinging them around like rag dolls. The riflemen sensibly retreated from their sandbags but the horn was blown again. A rumble could be heard throughout the town as riding down towards the town were Fomorian warriors mounted on Pucas. As these giant horned horses approached, soldiers tried to rush back to their sandbags, only to be attacked again by the enchanted wire. Taking careful aim, a sniper in one of the houses targeted the witch, causing the wire attack to stop. It was already too late because the cavalry had charged through the barricades. Some of these creatures were killed by machine guns but their riders loosed arrows, shooting at any soldier they could see. Black hounds which ran alongside the Fomorians attacked the machine gunners, tearing through their flesh. Soldiers fired from the houses as the Fomorians came charging in.

At the town centre, General Maloney was watching the Fomorian riders charging in. One of them snarled at him with its fangs but rather than being afraid, Maloney took out his pistol and fired it at the rider, killing the Fomorian. He continued to target the riders but soon ran out of ammo. He was in the process of reloading when he got knocked down to the ground. He stumbled out of the way of a trampling Puca as its rider tried to plunge her spear into him. Suddenly, a bang could be heard in the church steeple followed by a bullet shooting into the rider's forehead, killing her. The General then stood up. That bullet had come from a sniper positioned in the church tower.

The village was starting to be retaken by the Irish as the army used their armoured cars to start mowing down the Fomorian riders. Supporting the armoured cars were trucks packed with riflemen and machine gunners. Suddenly, a Fomorian dragon swooped down upon the town. Quincy managed to get the General out of the way as the dragon spewed flame upon a truck packed with riflemen. The truck burst into fire as the soldiers fled, screaming as they burnt. Riflemen fired at the dragon but weren't able to get at the belly. Winged Fomorians like the ones who had attacked the group in Elfland swooped down upon the townsmen.

As he saw them swoop down and try and pick up people, the General shouted angrily.

"Well, Mr. Harker, where is that army of yours?"

Before Quincy could answer, the thundering sound of automatic cannons could be heard coming from the nearby coast. The winged Fomorians that were terrifying the village suddenly got shredded. Surprised, the townsfolk and soldiers cheered as twin-engine jets swooped over the town. The children came running out of their homes to see the jets swooping overhead much to their parent's chagrin. Seosamh rushed outside calling to Sarah.

"Come on, Mam, I want to see the jets…"

Looking up in awe, Seosamh could see the larger four engine assault planes bristling with machine guns.

As the Fomorians regrouped and swooped in for another attack, a P.E.C squadron leader received the news on his radio.

"Bogeys coming in fast! Over?"

"Got it! We do this the old way! Break up and fire at will! Over and out!"

All the jets regardless of size broke out of formation and blazed their machine guns upon the creatures. Using computerized tracking systems, the assault planes were able to track the bellies of Fomorian dragons so as to take them down. The fierce battle that had broken out in the skies looked so distant and clean from the ground below but up for the pilots themselves it was dangerously close. The armoured airships helped to make the battle easier, using their heavy ordnance and missiles to provide covering fire for the jets.

Down below, the fight had become equally blood curdling as the P.E.C tanks had arrived and did battle with the Fomorian hordes. Though smaller than the Fomorian trolls and giants, the tanks were able to gun them down with their big turrets. Supporting the tanks were gunships and gyrocopters. The gyrocopters swooped across the battlefield dropping grenades on the Fomorians. In response, the Fomorian riders shot up at them with bows and arrows, striking some of the copters down. Peering through his binoculars, General Maloney was forced to make an admission.

"Well, when I was young, I never thought I'd be glad to see a foreign army in Ireland!"

"You will always have friends no matter how small, never assume that you are alone in your troubles."

As Quincy said this, Donacagh's airship could be seen in the sky, its propellers blowing away the clouds. Donacagh made the sign of the cross as he looked down at the battlefield from its balconies. He even personally manned one of the airship's guns to take out Fomorians.

Down below, the Druids had arrived with their own armoured vehicles and did battle with the Fomorians. The combined might of the Druids and P.E.C allowed the humans to begin encircling the Fomorian army on the ground but the Fomorians refused to yield, making the humans pay as much as possible for any gains. As the band of heroes flew across the battlefield in their gunship, Eric took out the Claíomh Solais. Clouds being blown away allowed the sun to shine through turning the grass from dull green to bright emerald. Taking advantage of this, Eric aligned the sword with the sunlight, allowing the sword to absorb its energy and then he unleashed a burst of light upon the Fomorian horde below, roasting a chunk of the Fomorians and causing many others to flee.

When they saw the glowing sword, the soldiers cheered and applauded Eric. However, Damien was focussed on his hometown in the distance. From what he could see, it had taken a beating from the Fomorian attack. Anguished, he turned to Bastian.

"Sir! That's my hometown down there, the faeries are still trying to attack it, we need to help my people!"

"Don't worry, Damien, we're coming!"

Meanwhile in the town, Donal could no longer restrain himself from venturing out of the house. Alarmed, Sarah called after him.

"Is the battle still going on?"

"Hang on, Sarah, I'm just going to check…"

His words were cut off as a winged Fomorian swooped down towards him. Startled, he stumbled, almost dropping his revolver. Horrified, Sarah ran after him to help him up. The Fomorian touched down between her and Donal and cracked its long spikey tail like a whip. Donal took aim with his revolver, but the creature knocked it out of his hand and pinned him to the ground. As it screamed at Donal, little did anyone know but Damien was in the gunship now hovering above the town. He trained his scoped rifle at the creature. Just as it was about to plunge its razor-sharp fangs into Donal's neck, a bullet shot straight through the creature. As it came out, it left a much broader wound in the chest of the winged Fomorian. Donal rolled out of the way as the creature stumbled to the ground. Looking up at the gunship that had been his salvation, Donal felt dizzy. Sarah anxiously helped him to his feet. He could hear the Fomorian horn blowing again, this time in retreat.

The gunship touched down a little distance away. The door opened and a ladder was lowered. Much to his surprise and his joy, Donal could see Damien emerging with a rifle, the rifle that had saved his life.

"Damien? Damien over here!"

"Dad? DAD!!!"

Damien ran so fast that he dropped his gun. Having not seen each other since Damien left for Dublin, Damien and Donal embraced. Sarah rushed over to clasp her son in her arms. Seeing Damien, the rest of the family were not long in joining in the embrace.

As he emerged from the gunship, Eric stopped to look at the happy family reunion. On one hand, he felt happy for Damien but on the other, he felt both a sense of grief and envy. Bastian emerged and observed the scene.

"Oh, you miss that, having a family you could cuddle up to, don't you?"

"I guess I do… I hope no human ever has to feel what I feel…that grotesque tragedy, the painful knowledge that you are the last of your race."

"Well....at least his parents are faithful, that's more than could be said about my mother who just left me and my father. There's something to be said about the poor of Ireland. They are devoted to each other despite their misery. They come to value what they have I guess; they don't have the time to be self-indulgent."

"I guess..."

"Trust me, I know all about it, Eric."

Bastian walked away, leaving Eric to look down at the sword, which seemed to have grown cold in his hand. Oisín nuzzled at his leg. Eric bent down to caress him. All around him, the humans were celebrating their hard-earned victory. They cheered as they saw the Fomorians flee.

That night, the once mostly quiet town was alive with music and laughter. Large crowds of both soldiers and townsfolk filled the pub to get drinks. Both P.E.C and the Druids had brought their own beers and cigarettes to share around. Donacagh, Phil, Bastian, Eric and Simon drank wine with the General. But Damien was happy to be in the pub with his family.

18

The Journey to Elf land

Back at the Druid base, several Druid guards stood watch around the cauldron. Their swords remained sheathed as they watched the place like hawks. Up on the balcony, more soldiers watched over the lab. For now, all was quiet. A guard made a cheerful remark to his comrade. "Did ye hear that we won the battle at Killala?"

"Oh, did we? That's nice to hear..."

A booming noise interrupted them. They looked at each other, alarmed. A flock of crows burst through the doors, disorienting them. Then, they vanished as suddenly as they had appeared. A voice they recognised boomed through the room.

"Did you think that was the end of my war, Druids?"

Coming back to their senses, they saw Brés standing in front of them. They drew their swords while the soldiers on the balcony raised their rifles. Brés' icy eyes glared at the Druids but then he smirked.

"I'm impressed, mortals. It was your kind, not mine that defeated the Tuatha De Danann in battle. A race of simian peasants such as yourselves managed to make this fortress, building structures more advanced than anything in Eire before. I sent all the nightmares that plagued your children against you and yet your species still stands and wins! Of course, all that will not mean much when you face Balor's great beasts of war!"

A guard pointed his sword at Brés and spoke sternly.

"We know well what your business here is! By order of Lord Donacagh O'Malley, this Cauldron is under the protection of the Society of Saint Patrick!"

"Oh, the Druids of Lord Donacagh O'Malley? How frightening... what can you do to stop me?"

The guard, enraged, charged at Brés....only for Brés to quickly brandish his own curved sword and parry the blow of the guard's broadsword. The guard maintained his courage and tried not to tremble.

"Brave sir! Do you not know your legends? No mortal weapon can strike me down. Mortal men, listen thoroughly and know that for every battle you win against me, my immunity to your weapons ensures that I will always be there..."

"We know painfully well that you enchanted yourself to be immune to our blades, false God! But if you seize that Cauldron, Eric, the incarnation of Lugh will come after ye with the Claíomh Solais! This Cauldron belongs to Ireland herself! By Saint Patrick we will not hand ye over the Cauldron!"

Brés sighed.

"Oh dear...poor fools...so be it!"

Brés chopped down the Druid guard without a sweat. This caused the other guards to yell out and charge all at once towards him. The soldiers opened fire with their guns but the bullets just bounced off Brés' body. All this didn't stop a soldier from alerting the rest of the base. But their bravery and courage was not enough to stop them from being slashed and sliced by Brés and soon every single one of the Druids guarding the cauldron was lying dead on the floor. As he flung the last Druid to the side, Brés strode up to the cauldron.

"Finally...."

Out in the corridors, soldiers rushed towards the entrance of the lab only for crows to come flying out at them. Some of the soldiers fired at the crows but as they did, the crows vanished. Entering the lab, they found not only that Brés had gone but that the troops they left to guard the Cauldron were all scattered lifeless across the floor. The Cauldron of the Dagda was nowhere to be seen. All of the men were stunned..

"My God....that was Brés....he has stolen the Cauldron of Dagda!" gasped an officer.

Turning to a soldier, he added.

"Send word to Lord Donacagh!"

The following morning, the sun had risen as life was slowly going back to normal and the P.E.C army was packing up its equipment. Eric, Simon and Phil were walking with Bastian when they heard a ship's horn in the distance. Simon turned to Bastian.

"Well, what do we do next?"

"We head for Elfland and for war. We stop Brés once and for all!"

"Only the Claíomh Solais can kill Brés, Elfland is a dreadful place, with monsters at every corner. The Fomorians will be able to do as they please with us!!"

"Lord Fitzgerald, the fact that Elfland is a death world crawling with monsters is exactly the reason we need an army, and a navy to head there!"

Quincy approached them.

"Well gentlemen? Are you ready for the invasion?"

Phil grinned.

"Well, we are getting a little old for this, but we're ready..."

As they turned back towards the town, Donacagh's voice could be heard roaring in anger.

"What? What do you mean it was stolen!!!"

They hurried over to the Druid position where Donacagh was on the phone. They felt a sense of dread as they listened to his side of the conversation.

"Brés? You mean Brés stole it?"

Phil looked at the others nervously.

"Eh....Brés stole what exactly?"

"I've a bad feeling we already know..." Simon whispered in reply. Donacagh was now shouting orders at whoever was on the other side of the line.

"Right! Guard the base, respond to attacks by Fomorian raiding parties and we'll get it back during our invasion!"

He slammed down the phone. Seeing the others standing there, he spoke in urgent and angry tone.

"Mr. Harker! I have ill news!! The Cauldron of the Dadga was stolen last night while we were out here partying!!"

"Stolen....but how??"

"Brés! Brés himself showed up at the base! Although repelling the attack on Killala was necessary I fear he used it as a diversion for his thievery! At this current moment, our army is superior to his in its capacity for war but should he resurrect Balor and his beasts of war, he will have an army that is immune to mortal weapons and he will be able to wipe us off Ireland entirely, plunging the island into an occupation that would make Cromwell look like a Faery godmother in comparison!"

Bastian frowned.

"By God....that bastard is smarter than I thought!!"

Quincy spoke urgently.

"We need to start assembling the invasion force, there is a gateway to Elfland out in the Atlantic, the only one large enough to move all our equipment into Elfland!! Come, we must move out, the sooner the better!"

The men moved out and soldiers, both Druid and P.E.C began to make their way to the shore. Having been contacted by Quincy, Giles had already sent transport ships to arrive at Ireland's shores so that the men could start loading their equipment. As they prepared to leave, Simon had a question for Eric.

"Shall we bring him?"

"Who?"

"Your young assistant, Damien?"

"I shall check but I have no intention of press ganging him."

Eric hurried to the O'Laoghaire's house. Little did he know but Damien had already anticipated the situation.

Damien, still dressed in his Druid uniform, was in the kitchen packing a backpack with various supplies, including food when Seosamh came to find him.

"You're packing up, Damien, where are ye going?"

"To Elfland, Seosamh....we're going to slay Brés, the Fomorian king who sent the attack on our town and who dragged poor Cillian into a bog."

"Wait a minute, ye are going to kill the king of the Fomorians? Damien, you are still only sixteen!"

"Well no, I'm not going to kill Brés, my boss, Eric Trent will do that."

"Then why are ye going?"

"Because we were there when the sword was dug up, our country was attacked as I made the journey back from Dublin, and....Seosamh....I've gone too far in this journey to just go back to normal. I don't think I can ever go back to normal."

"So...ye....ye are leaving us again, Damien?"

Seosamh looked sadly as Damien slung his backpack around his shoulders. Damien sighed as he turned to Seosamh.

"Listen, Seosamh, if the Fomorians are allowed to do as they please, Brés' army will return even stronger and there will be no home! Ireland will be conquered only twenty-three years after it became a Free State!"

Seosamh and Damien embraced. Seosamh's voice was a little

unsteady when he spoke again. "So, this is your job now, right?"

"Well, I don't know, if the battle we just had doesn't put our town on the map, I don't know what will."

Damien fitted his visored cap back on and slung his scoped rifle over his shoulder as he went outside the door. Although he appeared firm in his goal, Damien's heart was heavy as he left the house. Outside, he found Eric talking to his parents.

"Well, Mr. Trent have ye come to spirit my son away again on your adventure?" asked Donal.

Eric wasn't sure how to respond in a way that wouldn't anger them. He was taking Damien to Elfland, not Dublin this time. However, before he could respond, he saw Damien

"It seems he has already made up his mind on this, Mr. O'Laoghaire."

Donal and Sarah turned around to see Damien standing there, fully geared for the journey. Seeing his son equipped with both a rifle and backpack, Donal's eyes widened.

"My God, so ye are going again without even a break?"

"The war's not over yet Mam and Dad, I'll take my chances in this upcoming fight! Dad, if ye are worried about me...can't ye come yourself? Ye fought in our war of Independence and the Civil war, Dad, surely ye still have fight in ye left, don't ye?"

"Damien, my boy, did you not see me in the battle we just had. That pagan monster would have killed me had ye not saved my life. Damien, I'm getting too old."

Damien embraced both his parents before heading to the gunship where the others were. Eric turned to Donal.

"Mr. O'Laoghaire, could you walk with me?"

Donal nodded and followed Eric.

The wind blew in from the ocean while Donal and Eric

walked along the cliff head. Below them, they could see the seawater transforming into white foam as it crashed against the rocks.

"Mr. O'Laoghaire, I need to tell you something."

"Well, ye've got my attention, talk to me."

"With all that you have now seen, would you believe me if I told you that I am Lugh? A reincarnation of the half Fomorian and half Danann prince that led his people into battle with the Fomorians all those long dark years ago in your history? Would you believe me if I said that I get visions from Danu, a goddess you probably know better as Cathleen ní Houlihan?"

Donal stood stock still. Having heard a voice speaking in the Queen's English tell him that he was a reincarnation of one of the Tuatha De Danann that he heard about in his grandmother's stories, all Donal could manage was a gasp.

"Alright? Why are ye telling me this?"

Eric revealed the Claíomh Solais but he clutched it against his chest to shield it from the Sun.

"You remember this...this is what I originally came for. I dug this sword up in the name of knowledge and scholarship and had no selfish intentions to use it further my personal goals or that of an empire."

"I remember I hated ye for coming here, Eric. I was furious because I was scared that ye would just leave us with nothing and claim the sword for yourself, leaving Ireland the way it was. But ye returned Damien home safely to me and his mother. Ye are the one to kill Brés?"

"As commanded by Danu herself...this sword belongs to her as does the Cauldron. There can be no greater honour to her than returning her cauldron. I have become linked to the sword in ways I didn't expect."

A shocking thought occurred to Donal.

"Ye are going to die? Aren't ye? Not many get hailed personally by

Ireland to her bidding, and very few live on afterward to tell the tale."

"I know…"

Eric bowed his head solemnly as Donal put his hand on his shoulder.

"May the Lord be with you, Lugh, ye prove yourself to be a fine man."

Eric nodded before he walked off, leaving Donal to look on with awe. Hurrying after Eric, who was headed for the gunship, Donal saluted both him and Damien. Eric saluted Donal back before boarding the gunship. They buckled themselves in while Oisín crawled under their seats. Phil now sat alongside an aeronaut to help fly the gunship. Bastian eyed Damien.

"So, you are coming with us, are you Damien?"

"Yes, sir. I'm ready."

Damien felt a surge of excitement as he heard the propellers starting to spin outside. The gunship took off and headed over the sea. Many more gunships, airships and helicopters headed out for the Atlantic while soldiers, both Druid and P.E.C boarded what looked like armoured container ships. The ships blew their horns before retreating from the coastline and heading out into the open ocean to re-join with the fleet.

As they headed out into the Atlantic, Damien looked down to see a fleet of ships arrayed in the waters below. It mainly consisted of battleships, destroyers and cruisers. Nothing was too different about them except for the fact that they had more advanced equipment than a regular navy would. The jets and helicopters landed on an aircraft carrier that looked to be larger than any ship Damien had ever seen before. The transport ships were essentially armoured container ships with the funnel and control centre at the back of the ship.

Little did Damien know but underneath the fleet were submarine cruisers with turrets mounted on them. However, what stuck out to Damien the most was that there was a ship at the centre of the fleet that looked to be different than any of the other ships. The craft was shaped like a small cruiser but instead of guns or turrets, it had a device that was mostly made up of what looked like antennas. He also saw a radar on the ship that was spinning and beeping. Baffled, he turned to the others.

"Boss? Lord Fitzgerald? Look at the boat down there, what is that thing?"

Reaching across to look down at the ship, Simon simply smiled.

"I believe that's our gateway to Elfland."

"What?"

"It's called a portal engine. In the 1930s, only a few years before my retirement from P.E.C, our drills were becoming too expensive to maintain so our command wanted a more permanent solution. Mr. Harker approached the famous scientist Nikola Tesla for a more efficient solution. With his help, we created this device which could manually open tears into otherworldly locations. However, he only allowed us to use the technology for defending the world against the supernatural...we were not to give it to any Empire, even the British Empire for uses against rivals."

"How does it work?"

Simon sighed as he shook his head.

"I don't know, I'm not a scientist, I'd be as clueless with the device as your folk would be. I intend on keeping my distance and letting the white coats do their job."

The gunship landed on a landing pad on the carrier. Everyone got out of the gunship, feeling the cold salty air from the Atlantic blowing against their faces. Damien looked up at the radar dish spinning on the control tower and the communication antennas on the mast of the craft. The whole thing left him speechless. All around him, engineers and ground crew were working while a voice spoke through the intercom giving orders to the crew. As he heard the smooth voice speaking through the intercom, Damien muttered to himself.

"Right....and I used to think the horse and cart was exciting to be in. I went from a village with gas lamps to this..."

Out of the control tower came an officer who approached the group.

"Lord Fitzgerald, I presume?"

Simon answered,

"Yes....Captain, it's me and this is my entourage. Eric Trent, Phil Rodgers and Bastian O'Connell..."

"Ah, splendid...and who is this young man with the scoped rifle?"

Being singled out like that by the captain made Damien's cheeks go as red as a tomato. Eric spoke for him in a calm, steady voice.

"This is my assistant, Damien O'Laoghaire from the village of Killala. He is a capable fellow and one I would trust with my life. He helped me dig up the Claíomh Solais and in turn, has allowed us to defeat Brés."

"I see...not bad for a peasant."

Turning to Damien, he continued briskly.

"Welcome aboard young man, I'm Captain Giles of the Pellucidar Expeditionary fleet. You are a credit to your race. Gentlemen if you could follow me please."

As they followed, Oisín trotted beside Damien who was reflecting on the attitude of the PEC officer.

"He doesn't seem to have too much of a high opinion of us Irish Celts, well, at least he's a professional at what he does. We'll give him that..."

They took an elevator to the control room.

"I hear from Mr. Harker that you got the Druids of Lord Donacagh on our side. Their soldiers are in our cargo ships and I even saw Donacagh's zeppelin in the distance from which he commanded his fleet of helicopters. The zeppelin is armoured and it's bigger than our most formidable airships."

Phil nodded solemnly.

"Yes, with some persuading and through the grace of Eric being a reincarnation of Lugh, the Druids are on our side. They are some fighters; you should have seen them at Killala. Very handy these gentlemen were, maintaining their discipline in the face of horror, the perfect army to invade Elfland."

"Indeed! And when you see the weaponry they brought with them, I mean it looks nastier than even the Wehrmacht, that's not bad for a race of peasants."

Oisín barked angrily while Eric frowned.

"On the contrary, the Celts are a very industrious people, much like us. Besides, the Romans saw us English folk as a race of spooky bog dwellers once upon a time, did they not?"

"Yes, but we civilized ourselves and built an Empire...come gentlemen."

The group followed him into the control room. Within this space, crewmen operated the controls and spoke into radios. Looking around, Damien could even see clunky computers being operated. Officers dressed in dark blue uniforms and peaked caps oversaw the whole process. Gazing around with satisfaction, Phil nudged Damien.

"Well, young O'Laoghaire, what do you think of it all?"

"I don't know what to say...only a year ago, the most formidable vehicle I encountered was a simple motorcar...now, I'm in a freaking aircraft carrier with devices that look like it came from a Jules Verne book..."

"Indeed, young gentleman, times change quickly. I tell you English lads are often as surprised by this equipment as you are, Damien."

Meanwhile, Giles approached the helmsman.

"Is everything ready, helmsman?"

"The fleet has been assembled, Captain!"

"Good, signal the fleet and take us to the Atlantic! That's where our scientists discovered the portal to Elfland!"

"Yes sir!"

19

The expedition enters Elfland

In the following days, the fleet in its full glory headed for the Mid Atlantic ridge. Every so often, aircraft scouted ahead. One night, Damien was on the balcony of the control tower looking up at the stars in the night sky, feeling the cold salty wind against his face. Gloves shielded his hands from the cold while a scarf was wrapped around his neck. Despite this protection, he felt chilly. Looking down at the water, he hoped that he would see a whale leap out of the water. Back in Connacht, he used to go to the cliffs so that he could see whales. He heard footsteps on the metal floor of the balcony. Eric was standing behind him with Oisín by his side.

"Are you nervous about the oncoming battle?"

Damien shivered and wasn't sure how to answer.

"Don't worry, it's okay to be scared when entering an otherworld. As you know my first experience in another world was in the mystical Hollow Earth. I was a boy…"

"How were ye allowed to travel on a P.E.C mission at that age?"

"I didn't travel at my own free will; I was taken by a vain countess who sought to bargain with the monsters that dwelt there. I still have the bitter memory of being on the verge of ritual sacrifice and just how traumatised I was for ages afterwards. Still, my mother was there, and she and my father retrieved me, brought me home to Paris and kept me safe. I was bed ridden for a week as a result of the whole experience."

"And yet, ye still travel to Elf Land, a place even more savage than Hollow Earth?"

Eric nodded seriously.

"Of course, we sons of Europe are not a foe that can be easily intimidated, not even Mother Nature's power can deter our quest for knowledge."

Somehow, Damien didn't feel convinced.

"Is there another reason ye came out here?"

"Damien, I see that you've come to love Oisín, your little siblings loved him and he's getting old."

Damien didn't like the way this was going.

"Mr. Trent, why are ye telling me this?"

Eric sighed.

"Damien O'Laoghaire....will you care for my dog in his elder days?"

Damien's eyes widened.

"But he's more than your dog, boss, he's your friend is he not? The only friend you have had since ye were a child!"

"Which is why I want him in safe hands. Oisín is a strong and steadfast creature, native to Ireland. I've only known you for a short while but I've come to trust you thoroughly."

A terrible fear suddenly gripped Damien.

"Oh no, boss? Are ye going to die?"

"It might be a possibility, if so please ensure that my dog is not mistreated and exploited as is the fate of many a glamorous creature."

"Of course, I'll care for your dog if I must but I don't want it to come to this…"

Eric smiled.

 "Damien, could you put your hand on my chest…"

"Eh…why?"

"I want you to hear something."

        Curious, Damien put his hand on Eric's chest. He felt Eric's heartbeat, that slow drum-like heartbeat, and it seemed to have the effect of making Damien feel calmer.

"Is that your heartbeat, boss?"

"Yes, it has the effect of calming people…it was a technique my mother taught me if I got distressed. My people, the Agarthans, believed that our ancestors spoke through our heartbeat."

"I see…we simply told stories of our ancestors around the fire."

Eric smiled again.

"Goodnight, Damien, enjoy the night while you can. We might be in Elfland for some time."

Eric walked back inside to head for his sleeping quarters. Damien followed alongside Oisín.

The following day the ship had paused in the middle of the Atlantic. Based on their calculations, they were now at the Mid-Atlantic ridge. All the officers of the various forces, including Lord Donacagh, travelled to the aircraft carrier because that was the flag ship. That afternoon, these officers were sitting in a briefing room. Quincy stood beside a blackboard, addressing them.

"Gentlemen, listen all and listen well for what I am about to say is of the most serious significance for this mission."

As he spoke, Giles was drawing what looked like a claw on the blackboard. Taking up a stick, Quincy pointed to the claw.

"Based on ancient sketches and drafts by Greek and Roman surveyors, we have been able to recreate the map of Elfland. As you can see, Elfland is shaped like a claw with the major cliffs extending like nails. Between each cliff is a bay. Our first course of business will be the deployment of troops within these bays. In doing so we will establish a foothold within Elfland from which we can punch towards the central fortress and besiege it. Eric's task is to slay Brés, but how long we stay may depend on the reaction of the creatures, whether they want to kill us or just want to be left alone."

As he said this, Giles drew a circle which symbolised the fleet and then three arrows pointing to each of the bays. Each bay was marked with an X symbol.

Quincy became more solemn as he said.

"Gentlemen, mark me...I'm not going to sugar-coat this for any of you and I don't want you tempting the men with false promises. This will not be the type of adventure found in a boy's book. For Elfland is a dark and twisted world where there is no daylight. Only the moon provides any natural light while creatures lurk around every corner. All plants are brambled, the insects are big and the local foods are poisonous to mortal bodies. Our planes will even fly slower in Elfland, slow enough to mount the roof and shoot rifles from them. Not even the Romans could hold Elfland. Their ninth legion tried and failed dramatically."

This chilled the hearts of all who listened but it didn't seem to put any of them off. Quincy continued urgently.

"Gentlemen...does anyone want to go home? More than any other venture that we have done in the history of P.E.C, you risk the possibility of never, I mean never ever, seeing your loved ones again. If anyone fears such a fate, there are helicopters awaiting to take them back to our central depot in Northern Ireland. Raise your hands if you are such a man!"

Nobody moved a muscle. It was as if, regardless of their feelings, they felt they had all gone too far to turn back. Seeing this, Quincy relaxed.

"Good! Gentlemen, carry on and relay these instructions to your men."

During the following hours, the officers returned to their ships. Phil Rodgers and his co-pilot Stephen transported Bastian and Simon to a cargo ship so that they could lead an army once more. When the men in the cargo ship saw Bastian arriving, they cheered. Many of them had either heard of his conquests or had served with him personally. Simon grinned.

"They are ready to follow you Bastian, just as they did in the Argonne Forest in 1917, in Hollow Earth and now on the way to Elfland in 1944. I believe they will follow you to the ends of the Earth."

Bastian grinned back.

"Just like old times, Fitz..."

Back on the carrier, Eric and Damien followed Donacagh to his helicopter. Oisín followed them both. Quincy approached them.

"Lord Donacagh? Do your men understand what is to be done?"

"Mr. Harker, should a quick strike force not be enough? All we have to do is kill Brés and the Fomorians will be thrown into disarray. They will not be able to coordinate without a king to control them. Must we waste so many men in an operation that should only require the death of one soul?"

"My Lord, Brés has achieved what he has done by distracting us with attacks. That is why he unleashed creatures upon Ireland in the first place, to distract us from defending its treasures from him. So, to defeat him, we are going to distract his army with an invasion while Eric heads for Brés."

"And what of Balor? If he is resurrected, our army will be destroyed utterly!"

"That is why we must get in there and disrupt the ritual! The less time we waste arguing, the more time we have to stop the ritual. Is that understood?"

Donacagh merely bowed.

"You can count on my army and my loyalty. Even when I am not on it, my airship and its crew will support you."

Donacagh, Eric, Oisín and Damien proceeded via helicopter to the zeppelin. Damien turned Eric.

"What do we do now, boss?"

"For now, we wait until this evening. Take a good look at daylight, Damien, it may be the last time you see it for several days!"

That evening, all the fixed winged aircraft and gunships were safely on the carrier, everything was in position and the fleet merely awaited the command. The portal engine was bustling with activity as scientists operated the computers. Technicians kept an eye on the machines themselves. The scientists wrote in calculations which the huge clunky machines processed. As the computers processed the calculations, something strange started to happen. As the crew watched, lights started to flash and beep on the control panels around the computers, causing technicians to back away from the devices. A scientist nodded in satisfaction.

"We've made a breach between our world and Elfland! It's caused a tear in our reality."

Outside, dark clouds started to gather as everyone watched from their ships. Donacagh was standing beside Eric.

"Mr. Trent, do they know what they are doing?"

"Don't be scared, they're professionals whose field is entirely based around studying these kinds of events. They come from the highest-ranking colleges of England, America, even France and Germany."

Damien was captivated by what was happening. As lightning struck the portal engine's antennas, it recoiled into the air and started to tear a whole in the space in front of them. This tear extended into a large pitch-black hole. Everyone looked in awe at what had happened. Damien felt a sense of dread because the whole thing was so unnatural.

In the carrier, Quincy gave his orders.

"Proceed, Captain Giles, proceed slowly..."

Quincy watched the fleet move closer and closer to the portal. The area became darker and darker as they entered through it. Soon the fleet was travelling through a void that looked like space. The crew couldn't see anything except what was in front of them. Seeing the pitch-black void around them, Quincy spoke again.

"Captain, we need some illumination."

"Yes sir."

The fleet illuminated the area around it with its spotlights. After a seemingly endless journey, they touched down in a dark ocean.

The ocean itself was still, not a single wave could be seen. The water was as dark as the night sky above. The submarines used their sonar to make their way through it. The only light came from a ghostly moon. A sense of dread gripped crewmen that were out on the deck.

"My God, Danny! You'd think we were in Lovecraft country!" whispered one to his mate.

"Yeah! Let's hope we don't meet Cthulhu, right Frank?"

In the distance, the men could see what looked like cliff heads which were being circled by crows. Nobody said a word as they approached the cliffs. At the top of the cliffs, they could see what seemed to be points of light.

20

The battle for the Cauldron

On the mainland, the Fomorians and their creatures had gathered around the enormous body of a giant figure. The sorcerers and witches of the Fomorians had lit torches as they circled around the body. Drums were beating and booming while four sorcerers brought the Cauldron of Dagda as Fomorian warriors formed a guard of honour for them. Brés wore a silvery crown on his head as he rode towards the ritual on his Puca. A warrior blew his horn to signal Brés' arrival and when they saw him, all the Fomorians cheered and roared while creatures flying above screeched. They raised their weapons and the black hounds at their side howled. The sorcerers lowered the Cauldron to the ground, bowing to Brés as he approached it. The Cauldron glowed as Brés approached it and all the creatures fell silent.

Brés reached out his bare hand and touched the Cauldron. At that, the Cauldron glowed even more fiercely and Brés felt his hand burning. It caused him to recoil his hand in pain. Looking at his now burnt fingertips, Brés muttered to himself.

"Hmmm....indeed. You won't submit to my will easily, will you now, my lovely and beautiful Ireland?"

Turning to a sorcerer, he roared.

"Begin the ritual!!"

The sorcerers lifted up the Cauldron once again and proceeded towards the body of Balor while a Fomorian witch thumped her torch against the ground. It let off a booming sound that echoed through the land and it was followed by other creatures banging their weapons and torches in answer. The black hounds howled and the dragons roared. Brés brandished his sword.

"Creatures of the night!! The hour of our victory is at hand!!! Balor will be resurrected!! And with him we will have his army!!!"

The creatures screamed and cheered as they heard this. They clanked their weapons even faster.

But then they heard a boom in the distance. All stopped what they were doing and looked up. A shell slammed into the ground and exploded. The explosion caused all the creatures to panic and flee. A Fomorian looked out towards the ocean to see P.E.C battleships firing their big guns at the coast. Seeing the brightly lit P.E.C vessels and airships in the distance, he murmured to himself.

"It cannot be..."

Turning to Brés, he announced.

"Sire!! The humans have entered Efland!!! They are here for the Cauldron!!!"

Brés glared in the direction of the coast and saw the smoke emitting from the ships in the bay.

A groan escaped him.

"Lugh"

He shook himself as he roared.

"To arms!!! Summon all the creatures of Elfland!!! Guard the Cauldron from the humans!!! Lugh has come with an army of men!!!"

The Fomorians scrambled for their weapons and rushed towards the coast where their towers of flame were located. Sorcerers manned the towers while longbowmen arranged themselves at the cliffs. Down on the beaches, Fomorian warriors arrayed themselves in shielded formations while dragons and winged Fomorians took to the sky.

Other Fomorians mounted their Pucas while trolls and giants reinforced the army. The sorcerers tried to shield their towers from the bombardment, but they were unable to shield those arrayed outside.

◆ ◆ ◆

Back at the fleet, the battleships continued to fire while the carrier was a hub of activity. Gunships powered up as they were boarded by heavily armed and armoured soldiers mounted with jet packs. Phil and Stephen climbed into the cockpit of a gunship.

The helicopters, both Druid and P.E.C took off and circled around Donacagh's zeppelin. Down below, the transports headed for the coast at full speed. While that happened, submarine cruisers burst out of the water and bombarded the cliff heads to kill off Fomorian archers before submerging again. The transports headed for the shore while gunships and airships flew above as escort.

As they saw the transports coming in, sorcerers sent fireballs from their towers at the incoming ships. These fireballs either crashed against the water, burning out or they slammed into the control tower of a transport. There, they triggered explosions in the engine which caused the whole ship to blow up. In such ships, fire spewed into the air as men leapt off the ship in agony. Watching the scene below from the cockpit of his gunship, Phil reached a conclusion.

"Something has to be done about these towers! Our aviation is being distracted by the dragons!"

"What are your orders, sir?"

"Come Stephen, let's give them a gift, shall we?"

"You mean jump troopers?"

"Precisely, those lads are spoiling for a fight!"

Phil carefully maneuvered the gunship so that its stern faced the tower. The sorcerer and the archers were so focused on firing at the transports that they didn't notice the gunship opening its ramps. Inside the gunship, jump troopers in oxygen masks and metal helmets activated their jet packs and darted out of the craft, swooping down onto the sorcerer's tower. One of the sorcerers heard the sound of gunfire and turned around to see Fomorian warriors being gunned down by the jump soldiers. Surprised, he powered up a fireball only for a jump soldier to blast him with a tommy gun. The jump soldier then continued to fight on with his comrades to repel the Fomorians that were closing in.

Up above, a battle was taking place as flying creatures led by dragons attacked the human Heli fleet, initially tearing through both Druid and P.E.C gunships. Observing from his airship, Donacagh turned to the captain of the zeppelin.

"Fire at will!!"

"Yes, my Lord!!"

The zeppelin blazed its machine guns around the place shredding through the flying creatures. The P.E.C airships followed suit and opened fire with their own guns. This covering fire allowed the Heli fleet to regroup and reorganise before striking out to attack again. Once they recovered, the helicopters broke formation and pursued the creatures. Jets showed up to support them in the escalating dogfight. However, there were so many Fomorian creatures attacking them that none of the squadrons could give covering fire to the transports below.

Down at the beach, a transport finally came to a halt. At first, the Fomorians awaited in formation with their archers at the ready. The ship's bow opened, revealing a ramp that came crashing down onto the beach. Suddenly the Fomorians heard Bastian's voice yelling out. "For God and for your country......ATTACK!!!!!"

The sound of the Druid bagpipers playing "Blue Bonnets" echoed across the land, followed by the roaring of men as both Druid and P.E.C soldiers came charging out of the transport.

Fomorian longbowmen fired down from the cliffs at the charging soldiers, slaying them and for now the Fomorian formations waited. But then they heard tracks clattering against the ground as a P.E.C heavy tank, with Bastian mounted on its turret came trundling out of the ship. The tank ignited its flame thrower, spewing flame into the Fomorian warriors, setting them alight. As a result of this, their formation disintegrated, allowing the human soldiers to gun them down. The archers tried firing at the tanks as they came onto the shore. Their arrows either just embedded themselves in the tank or fell off them while soldiers fired up at the cliffs. Similar scenes were taking place all across Elfland as the humans gained a foothold.

The Fomorian formations quickly collapsed to bombardment by tanks and missiles meaning that by the time the human soldiers came, there was little resistance. Seeing the Cauldron glowing in the distance, Simon's eyes widened as he watched from the tank alongside Bastian. He shouted to the men.

"Secure the Cauldron!!! Head for the Cauldron and secure it for extraction!!!"

Monsters and creatures climbed up onto the tank as Simon brandished his sword, hacking through the creatures. Bastian also killed such creatures, hacking them in two with his machete.

Fomorian sorcerers and witches attempted to strangle the charging soldiers with brambled vines and thorns. Some of these brambles even tried to wrap around Bastian and Simon who slashed the brambles with their blades.

The tank they were on fired its cannon at a troll while rockets fired from one of the Druid rocket artillery vehicles struck the group of sorcerers and witches, causing an end to the brambles and thorny vines.

At first Brés fought, slaying humans that approached him in a brutal manner. A crow flew close to him.

"The battle is going ill for us, sire!! The humans are encroaching on the Cauldron!!! I suggest that…."

For answer, Brés merely teleported himself back to his fortress so that if Eric were to come for him, he would have to wade through all its defences. Without the presence of Brés, many monsters, especially the badly treated grunts, fled back to their caves, deserting the Fomorian cause.

Phil's gunship swooped over the battle strafing Fomorians. Phil and Stephen kept their eyes firmly on the battle below.

"Well Stephen, Elfland isn't as scary as it was the last time we came here! Right?"

"Yes, indeed, it helps that we have much more firepower!"

Neither of them were aware that a dragon was flying up behind them. However, the dragon was noticed by a jeep with two bazookas whose crew trained their rockets on it. The men fired a rocket from one of their bazookas in an attempt to strike the dragon but the missile, being fired too early, slammed into the tail propeller of the gunship causing it to spin violently out of control.

In the cockpit, alarms went off and lights flashed.

"Stephen?? Stephen…what in the name of God just happened?"

"We just got hit by a missile!"

"Hang on, Stephen, we must try to regain control!"

The crew panicked as they tried to bail out of the gunship. The dragon burnt them. Seeing the chaos that they had accidentally caused; the jeep soldiers were horrified and they fired another missile at the dragon. This time they were able to strike the dragon, knocking it down to the ground. The gunship spun till it slammed into the ground, skidding across the terrain as it got ripped apart until only the cockpit remained. Phil was alive, but his face was bloodied as he pulled off his helmet. As he sat up, he muttered furiously.

"I'm going to shoot those hooligans myself for knocking us out of the sky…"

He then turned to Stephen saying,

"Come on, sunshine, there's still fight in us yet, let's…."

Phil tugged at Stephen, then noticed that Stephen's eyes were closed. Letting go, he saw Stephen's body slump down and his head fall against the control panel. Sticking through Stephen was a huge piece of iron.

Phil slammed his fist against the controls as he shouted tearfully.

"Well, here ends the ballad of Stephen McQuaid, to have followed me all the way from some little town in Donegal!! Only to be hit by a missile from Boston!"

Phil patted Stephen on the shoulder. He then burst out of the cockpit yelling.

"Aim straight and properly, you bastards!!!"

Surrounded by the battle going around him, Phil felt dizzy. By now, the humans were starting to secure the Cauldron but Phil stumbled to the ground beside the cockpit where he lay for a prolonged period. Two giant black hounds approached him. Just as they were about to take a bite out of him, gunfire scared them off, followed by the clattering of tracks.

The spotlights of Bastian's tank shone upon Phil. The tank came to a halt as Simon shouted.

"Phil? Bastian, it's Phil Rodgers!!"

Simon and Bastian got off the tank as Phil groaned. He felt dizzy and unstable as he opened his eyes. Bastian called to Simon.

"Simon, get the med kit from the tank..."

He then turned to a crewman.

"Get a medic, do it now!"

Bastian leaned over Phil to check to see if he was still breathing. Soldiers surrounded them to give them cover as they tended to Phil.

21

The Final Clash

Looking down on the battle that was going on below, Eric felt encouraged.

"Good Lord, Donacagh, I haven't even used the sword of light and we are already winning the battle for Elfland!!"

Donacagh was less sanguine.

"Yes, but that victory will only be temporary until Brés himself is slain…"

"Indeed, where is he? You would imagine he would be fighting with his warriors. It's not like he has nothing to fear!"

"Oh Eric, you forget that Brés has no sense of honour. He's happy to screech and rile other beasts into battle, have them spill their blood against our blades and bullets while he sits on his throne, waiting for the next time he can strike against men."

Eric's voice was full of contempt.

"Well Lord Donacagh, we must advance on the fortress. A coward like that should not be allowed to live!"

Looking out from the Zeppelin's cockpit, Eric could see that the fortress was built into a mountain and surrounding it was a spiked wall ranked with sorcerer's towers. Donacagh called to him.

"Eric! Come with me…we cannot succeed in this endeavour without you!"

Eric, understanding what he had to do, followed Donacagh. Before they left the bridge, Donacagh appealed to his soldiers.

"My brothers! We strike at the heart of this evil! Which one of you will follow me?"

A group of Druid soldiers, including Fionn, followed Donacagh. Seeing this, Oisín and Damien followed. Slinging the rifle over his shoulder, Damien caught up with Eric.

"Hey, wait, where are ye going, Mr. Trent?"

"What does it look like, O'Laoghaire? We're heading to fight Lord Brés. I suppose you are coming, are you?"

"I've gone too far to step down, boss, I'm coming with ye."

Eric, Damien, Donacagh, Fionn and Oisín climbed up to the ladder to reach the landing pad, escorted by soldiers. Eric tapped Damien on the shoulder..

"You've gotten rather comfortable with aviation, haven't you, Damien?"

"A helicopter is not the same as a plane, besides I eat a lot less since I realized we'd be flying to locations rather than walking or driving there!"

Eric grinned as he heard the engine power up. As the propellers of the helicopter began to spin, Donacagh gave his orders to the pilot.

"Take us to the fortress, it's time we end this battle and slay this tyrant once and for all!"

The helicopter took off from the zeppelin and flew towards the fortress, completely ignoring the battle going on around them. The zeppelin continued to fight on, barraging the most menacing and largest dragons with its missiles.

Down below, the Cauldron of the Dadga, still glowing, was now secure in the hands of the humans. Human soldiers were fortifying the area around the Cauldron with sandbags and machine gun emplacements. Tanks, airships and gunships also provided support.

As they manned a turret on one of the vehicles, some soldiers looked up to see the Druid helicopter flying towards the fortress. They pointed at the craft, dumbstruck by the sight of seeing a lone copter flying straight towards the fortress. A soldier called to Bastian.

"Sir! Look up!"

Bastian turned to Simon.

"Is that Donacagh and Eric?"

"I presume so, may God be with them both!"

Bastian turned to a radio operator.

"Contact the fleet!! Send them the coordinates of the fort!! That team needs fire support!!"

"Yes sir!"

Turning to the rest of the soldiers, Bastian continued.

"Gentlemen!! We need to guard the Cauldron and distract Brés' army!! Defend the Cauldron and ensure that it doesn't get into enemy hands!!"

"Yes sir!"

The battle between humanity and the Fomorians continued.

Up above, Donacagh's team flew over the walls. Sorcerers hurled fireballs at the helicopter, but missed because it was going so fast. Damien shot at the sorcerers in an attempt to kill them but wasn't too sure if he was succeeding. It didn't matter too much because the towers themselves were being blown up by munitions fired by the battleships out at sea. As they got closer, longbowmen fired at the helicopter. However, the arrows only bounced off the craft. The helicopter reached a balcony and blazed its machine guns, slicing through all the archers gathered there. The craft lowered a ladder so that the squad could enter the fortress. It was a long uphill battle as the team fought their way through the corridors to the throne room, and several Druids were slain in the process. As they reached the big doors of the throne room, the Druid soldiers set up defence positions around the entrance. Donacagh turned to Eric.

"This is it, Eric, what happens in that room will define the fate of Ireland herself!"

"I'm aware of that, my Lord....keep this room covered while I slay Brés!"

In the large dark throne room, rows of torches ran down on either side from the throne. At the centre of this throne, Brés pressed his hand against his head as he sat hunched over. Crows perched themselves above the bramble infested throne while gunfire could be heard in the distance. Suddenly, the great doors were yanked open as Eric shoved them apart. The Claíomh Solais glowed, causing Brés to feel fear for the first time. His heart thumped as he saw the glowing sword come closer. Eric strode forward towards the throne.

"Are you just going to sit there....in the dark? Your creatures are dying to men's weapons all because of a war you, not they, not I, but **you** started! Must they suffer for your arrogance? For men's weapons are immensely superior to yours."

Hiding his fear of Eric behind a smug tone, Brés replied.

"Men, Lugh, are you going to rely on mortal men to stop me? Men may be more powerful and yes, they were able to stop me from resurrecting Balor. But though their weapons have changed much, they are as weak willed and as divided as ever. Just like in Arthur's time, mortals blindly follow the shepherd who feeds them well and gives them false promises..."

"As if you are any different, Brés, you too give false promises to beasts to make them die stupidly."

Brés stood up from his throne.

"I don't need to wipe out the race of mortal men, Lugh, with weapons like that in the hands of weak minds, they will wipe themselves out. And when their world has burned, then I will arise and..."

"You won't live to see that day!"

Eric took off his long coat and rolled up his sleeves of his white shirt. He then readied the Claíomh Solais.

Seeing the glowing sword, Brés stepped down from his throne, shaking off his fur cloak and revealing his topless rune patterned body. He drew his own curved sword.

"So be it, Lugh...let this be your end, son of Eire!"

"Fine, and if it is Ireland's wish...let this be your end as well!"

For a long moment, neither moved. Then, in a burst of energy they clashed blades. There was no glamour in this fight, the men kneed each other, wrestled each other, kicked each other and elbowed each other as they parried their blades.

Outside the throne room, Damien and Oisín could hear the sound of swords clanging. Oisín whined softly and looked up at Damien.

"I know what ye are thinking...come on, let's find out what's going on in there!"

Damien and Oisín rushed into the throne room as the Druid soldiers including Donacagh fought off the attacking Fomorians.

The duel continued for a prolonged period but then Eric knocked Brés' sword out of his hand. Brés seemingly allowed Eric to lunge at him, but then he ducked Eric's thrust as he shouted.

"No!"

Unsheathing a knife from his belt, Brés plunged it into Eric's hip, causing Eric to stop. Damien gasped in horror and Oisín howled as Eric suddenly stumbled face down on the ground. Overjoyed, Brés turned Eric over to finish him. Eric tried to get up but Brés stomped on his chest.

"Do you think I would have played fairly with you, Lugh? Playing fair makes you lose...the Fomorians learnt it, the humans learnt that lesson but you, your fair skinned race from Thule, you never learnt, that is why you died out..."

Brés reached down and scratched him with his clawed hand.

"You are the last of your race...are you not? Even if you win this day, you would just rot with time, for you would be neglected, abandoned and eventually alone. You would be just like me. So, consider this death a favour for you, brave but stale son of Danu."

Brés knelt down with his knees on either side of Eric as he raised his knife. As he readied to plunge it into Eric's throat, Damien readied his rifle and shot it at Bres, but the bullet merely bounced off. Brés scowled and spun around to see Damien.

"Well, well, well!!! What is it we have here?? A mortal man? Not just any kind of mortal...the human peasant from the dirty bog infested lands that make up Connacht!! You, a smelly commoner, have the gall to disrupt our duel??"

Brés laughed and sneered at Damien as he bent to pick up his sword. Furious, Damien fired his gun at him again. He knew it had no effect, but it still distracted Brés. Already, behind him, Eric began to stand up, and using what remained of his strength, he clenched the Claíomh Solais.

Brés continued to taunt Damien.

"You inferior fool, no mortal man can kill me, let alone a bog barbarian such as yourself!"

Damien simply spat at him.

"Does that spell work on dogs? Go get him Oisín, make sure he swallows his pride!"

Oisín growled as he leapt upon Brés, clawing and biting at him. Brés flung Oisín off but the dog got back up and came at him again.

"You petty beast, I'm not going to let you get away with that easily!!"

Brés raised his sword to chop Oisín in half, only for Eric to come at him from behind. Eric yelled out as he plunged the sword of light through Brés' body. Seething with anger, Eric shouted at a shocked Brés.

"Maybe if you weren't so egotistical and wasteful, Ireland might be Elfland once more!"

Brés still had both his eyes and his mouth wide open with shock as Eric yanked the sword out of him. Eric then shoved the Fomorian king to tumble face flat on the ground. At first, Damien was about to cheer for he couldn't believe his eyes. He was gripped by an awe at the possibility that something very ancient and powerful had finally been vanquished. But then he noticed with dread that Eric was starting to sway. Then, he collapsed to the ground.

"No!!!" Damien forgot everything as he ran over to Eric where he now lay gasping for breath. Barking frantically, Oisín also ran over.

Suddenly, all over Elfland, a sudden change took place. A Fomorian chieftain took out his horn and blew it. All of a sudden, the creatures of the night fled and retreated to their caves leaving the humans bewildered. This silence was broken by the men cheering and celebrating. Bastian seemed to be utterly dumbstruck.

"What? What just happened?"

Simon looked around at the empty landscape.

"It seems that Bres has been slain. With him dead, the creatures of the night are no longer bewitched into serving him. Thus, they are no longer fighting us, I guess."

Bastian turned to Phil and Simon.

"Then come on! Let's get to the fortress, if Brés has been slain, I want to see it for myself."

Simon's eyes were clouded by anxiety.

"But I fear he is not the only one."

◆ ◆ ◆

Damien felt a sense of pure dread as he leaned over Eric.

"Boss....Boss?"

He tried to raise Eric from the ground. Oisín licked Eric's cheeks.

Eric's voice was faint as he tried to reply.

"Ah Damien…"

"Oh, but Eric, ye are getting cold, isn't your species supposed to generate warmth?"

"Yes, but I am dying, Damien, my life on this earth is coming to an end."

Damien gasped.

"Oh no!! But ye are still young, ye still have a life, Eric, please don't……"

"Ah, my physical body is still young, yes, but my heart aches with age, for I have grown weary of the same struggles repeating themselves again and again…I live with the memories of my past life."

Damien's eyes stung and his face grew red.

"Oh Eric, what do you want me to do?"

Eric grasped Damien's shoulder.

"Hear me, Damien, when I am dead, place me upon a pyre…burn me, burn my body at the cliff heads of Killala and let the winds of the Atlantic scatter my ashes into the water! So that I may return to the sea from where all life emerged!"

"Oh, but Eric, ye shall not live to see me marry, live to see me have a child, ye shall never live to see your victory and our celebration of it nor shall ye see my hometown prosper…"

Eric touched Damien's cheek.

"Damien, you must forge your own path. Your father must be a lucky man to bear a child such as you for you would exactly be the kind of child I would love to have had. No, do not weep…the angels are already here."

Eric bright glowing blue eyes closed one last time.

Distraught, Damien pressed his hand against Eric's chest, feeling for his heartbeat. The drum-like sounds of Eric's heart beating came to a sudden halt and then there was silence. Oisín's nostrils sniffed and twitched and then he howled in sorrow. Damien knelt down beside Eric's corpse and slowly removed his cap and bit his lip so as to stop himself from crying. The harder he tried, the more he found that he couldn't hold back and he sobbed as he hugged Oisín. He didn't even know what to do next when suddenly he felt a powerful, haunting and yet gentle presence and saw a glowing pale hand on his shoulder.

Looking up, Damien saw Danu herself standing there. He gasped because even though he had never seen Danu for himself, he had heard enough to figure out that this presence was her. She spoke in a firm but gentle voice.

"Brés may never have been stopped had you not stopped him from killing Lugh….thank you for being so brave and strong."

Damien, feeling both exhausted and heart wrenched, stumbled into her arms. When the Druids came in, they saw Danu too. Seeing her, they all took off their helmets and kneeled in honour of her, as did Donacagh.

A few days had passed and a crowd of people had gathered around the cliff head at Killala. Everyone from the Druids, to P.E.C, the regular Irish troops and even the villagers from Damien's hometown were present. They stood to attention as they watched their priest perform burial rites before a wooden pyre. Resting upon the wooden pyre was the body of Eric Trent, wrapped in a tartan robe. The Claíomh Solais was clasped firmly in Eric's hands and it still glowed.

Damien watched alongside Oisín and his family as a Druid

guard approached the pyre. When the priest finished the prayers, the guard lowered the torch and tipped it against the pyre. The pyre then began to light up as more torches were applied to it. A piper played a lament as the funeral pyre began to blaze. Looking up, Damien could see Danu in the distance, smiling solemnly as she faded away. Seeing her fade, Damien smiled to himself. When the burning was done, the Druids took the Claíomh Solais back to their base where it would be stored safely.

Later that day, Damien and Donal walked together near the town. Donal was well aware of his son's emotional upheaval.

"Ye are going to miss him, aren't ye?"

"I know, it's weird, I only knew him for a few weeks, I guess and yet..."

"Damien, I had a talk with your Mr. Trent. I'm pretty sure he knew he was going to die. Can't blame ye, he was a great man and he actually kept his promise!"

"I know."

Donal changed the subject.

"Still, you have this huge sum of money now, because from what I hear as Eric has no heirs to his inheritance, Lord Fitzgerald is redistributing the money to you as reward for fighting the Fomorians..."

When Damien heard that, he felt very uncomfortable, for he increasingly understood that money was as much a curse as a blessing. Before he could respond, his father continued in a more urgent tone.

"Damien, answer me this, are ye going to dart off to Dublin again with that money? You can live as easily as the Norman lords that once ruled this country."

Damien turned to face his father.

"No, Dad, that money is too much for one man, this money needs to be used for the good of our town. As ye said Dad, this town is dying and if I can help give it life, I will."

Donal laughed with pleasure.

"Well, Damien, you're not even eighteen yet and ye already think like a grown man. Still, there's a lot of objects left behind by the Fair folk, if that won't put our town on the map, I don't know what will."

The two laughed as they continued their walk back to the town.

EPILOGUE (1954)

Ten years had passed since the battle of Killala and it was as if nothing ever happened. The sun was shining brightly over the emerald grass upon the cliff head and seagulls flew overhead. The salty waters of the Atlantic rose up and crashed against the rocks before retreating from the pebbles and sand on the beach below, such a scene was timeless. Except this time, a much older Oisín was perched beside a little boy that bore a remarkable similarity to Damien himself, including his nut-brown hair. He turned his head at the sound of his father's voice.

"Eric? Eric, come here."

Eric O'Laoghaire ran back to his father. Damien was now a man of twenty-six and was a very different person than he had been at sixteen. He wore a light brown long coat over his suit and a fedora on his head. His hair was short, smooth and tidy while his face was still beardless. Beside Damien was a pretty young woman with a slim body, icy white skin and thick wavy raven hair that tumbled loosely over her shoulders. She had a furry blue coat wrapped around her body, a scarf around her neck and a bonnet on her head.

As Damien put his arm around her shoulders, she gazed around with sapphire blue eyes.

"Is this where it all started? Ye digging up the most magical sword in Ireland to get some money."

"Aye, Siobhan, it is, although it was Seosamh's idea to go digging up the sword. As you know, he's now gone to America. I believe he has made a new attraction at Disney known as the "Elfland ride". Feels stupid looking back, we basically started a war...then again, I was hungry back then and you don't think straight when ye are hungry."

"Look on the bright side, Damien, we wouldn't have met if you hadn't used that money for your studies. Then my father took an interest in the exhibition that was hosted at your town; I believe it's why he paid your town a visit."

Damien smiled.

"I know. Again, that was Seosamh's idea. Still, it's probably thanks to his visit that I found my way into the civil service and more importantly, that's how I met ye."

As he said this, he wrapped his arms around her. Looking over her shoulders, Damien could see the large electric pylons decorating the region while cars and buses now drove along the roads. Eric tugged at his father's coat. Damien lifted him in his arms. The O'Laoghaires were about to return to their car but Eric was pointing to something far out at sea. Curious, Damien passed Eric back to the warmth and security of his mother's arms. In the distance, a gigantic whale leapt up into the air. The whale displayed its flippers in their full glory before plunging back down into the water, much to the joy of the O'Laoghaires as they watched together.

Behind them, Damien's hometown was bustling with activity. It was a lot less quiet than it had been during the Emergency. Damien would never forget the day that changed his life forever. The day when the Agarthan stranger came looking for the Claíomh Solais.

CLAÍOMH SOLAIS
BACKGROUND LORE
AND INSPIRATIONS

Basic introduction

The first thing to be said about the "Claíomh Soláis" is that it is a work of fiction and not a historical text. It can be best described as taking inspiration from a mixture of genres that shaped both Irish and British cultural history, most notably Christianized versions of the pre-Christian Celtic mythology, the Anglo-Irish Gothic novel as well as the "scientific romances" of the late 19th and early 20th century. It also takes some level of inspiration from the historical context of Ireland during the early to mid-20th century (including the second world war). What I'm laying out below is background lore exploring the different elements that play a role in the Claíomh Solais.

Ireland in the early 20th century

It would probably take a very skilled historian to truly explain the political context of Ireland in the early 20th century, the context in which our protagonist Damien O'Laoghaire grew up. Ireland, unlike most countries in Western Europe started the 20th century as a colony, a colony of the British Empire. Ireland itself was divided into two major groups, one was that of an anglicized Ireland that was Protestant and sought to maintain the Union between Ireland and Britain and the other which was a nationalist cause seeking to both revive the original Irish speaking Gaelic culture as well as initiate a rebellion against the British Empire to secure Independence. (Important note: The nationalists initially sought home rule in which Ireland merely had control over its domestic affairs but eventually this developed into a call for full independence.)

During World War 1, Ireland was promised Home Rule if Irish men fought in the British army. However, in 1916 the Easter Rising, led by Patrick Pearse and others led to a week-long battle that ended in the uprising being suppressed and the leaders being executed. This not only postponed Home Rule, but the mass executions also led to a backlash against British rule. This meant that although Ireland did get a parliament in 1918 after the end of the First World War, due to seeking independence and also due to being treated badly by the British authorities, the Irish continued to initiate an armed resistance that this time, was led by Michael Collins who was eventually able to succeed in gaining Ireland some level of independence in 1921 through the Anglo-Irish treaty. But this led to a civil war because it only secured the southern part of the island and not the North. Though the Free State survived and won the Civil war, the divisions of this treaty still linger in Irish politics to this very day.

The "Emergency"

World War 2 does not need explaining as it is probably the best known and most destructive conflict in the history of the human race. Therefore, it may be surprising to readers unfamiliar with Irish history, that the Second World War doesn't feature much within the Claíomh Solais, despite the fact that the story takes place in 1944, the year of the D-Day landings that would free France and the rest of Europe from Nazi Germany would take place. But it is important to note that Ireland was a neutral country during the Second World War. In Irish history, this period was known as the "Emergency". To sustain this neutrality, any news about the war was censored by the State and every good from petrol to even tea was rationed. Still Ireland was biased towards the Allies, helping any RAF pilots that crashed in Ireland to make their way over the border back to the North.

Ireland itself was a poor country and the rationing that came as a result of the war made life only harder for the Irish people. Ireland in the early 20th century was officially a democratic state but it could in many ways be classed as "theocratic" in that the Catholic church, particularly under Archbishop Charles McQuaid and when De Valera was in office, was a dominant influence. This was because the Church ran most institutions within the country from the hospitals to the schools, they also censored any text that could be considered "obscene" (not too differently from our own modern "outrage culture", this term was broad and it was applied to a wide variety of cultural texts ranging from books to films). Despite this, Ireland was still a successful and functioning democracy in which all adult citizens could vote. More importantly it managed to survive the turmoil that normally tormented postcolonial countries in their early days of independence without collapsing into constant civil disorder.

Despite attempts to get the economy into motion, and certain forms of modernization such as the use of electricity, life for the average Irish citizen was hard, particularly in the rural regions in the West where it was difficult to grow crops. Large numbers of Irish still left the country to seek opportunity elsewhere with many filling the ranks of both British and American armies during the war. Indeed, all too often, films made at this time such as "Man of Aran", "Darby O'Gill and the Little People" and most famously "The Quiet Man" tended to depict these rural regions as this Arcadian ideal in which the people were free from the "evils" of mechanized "Modernity". The reality was quite the opposite...it was a world defined by poverty and brute hardship.

Celtic Culture and Christian influences

The Celts were an Indo-European people that conquered and populated most of Europe including Ireland in Antiquity. Most of this Celtic Europe got conquered by the Roman Empire and then later by Germanic tribes such as the Teutons, Anglo-Saxons, Goths and Franks. Both those cultures (Roman and Germanic) would shape the image of European society in the coming centuries. Ireland continued to remain independently Celtic even with Christianization until the Middle ages. The Celts of Ireland would then get invaded first by the Pagan Norse and then by the Norman Lords of England which would pave the way for English occupation of Ireland in the following centuries.

Irish society was originally a polytheistic society which worshipped many Gods. Little is actually known about what pagan Ireland was really like. What is known is that it had a hierarchical and monarchic culture and that its priests were known as the Druids and that it was a network of different feuding tribes. History among the Celts was relayed orally by the Bards and also through Ogham, a system of writing. Irish Celtic warriors used iron to make their weapons, thus giving the Celts an advantage over cultures that used bronze. In the late years of the Roman Empire, Ireland was Christianized by the Welsh missionary Saint Patrick who became its patron saint. It is important to note that when Celtic Irish mythology was being written down, it was written by Christian monks whose versions of the myths had Christian themes inserted into them. This includes the breaking of pagan curses by Christian priests and the idea of the faeries being demons.

The Tuatha De Danann, the Fomorians and Agartha

The "cycle of invasions" was a text that was written in the Middle Ages in Ireland that was a Christianized account of five mythical invasions that happened in Ireland. Perhaps the most notable for this story was the fourth invasion of Ireland by the

"Tuatha De Danann". The Tuatha De Danann were a race of magical superhuman beings that were tall, fair skinned and who had either red or blonde hair. These beings ruled Ireland but then clashed with a mythical race of monsters known as Fomorians. However, though the Tuatha De Danann drove out the Fomorians, the Tuatha De Danann were displaced by a race of humans with iron weapons known as the Milesians. These people are said to be the ancestors of Irish people and were credited as being one of the races of men scattered by God as a result of the tower of Babel.

Names such as Lugh, Bres and Balor come from the Irish myths. In the "Claíomh Solais", the Tuatha de Danann were a tribe of "Tileans", a superhuman Aryan race from the pre flood world of Thule of which Eric is the last. The idea of a superhuman race creating an advanced civilization, only to be destroyed by a Great Flood emerges particularly in Victorian occultism in the late 19th century, for example in the book "Atlantis: The Antediluvian world" by Ignatius Donnelly. Also emerging in Victorian occultism is the myth of Agartha, which was believed to be a great city within the Earth that would open its gates when humanity lived up to the Ten Commandments properly. The Tileans in this story are both the ancestors of the Tuatha De Danann and the ones who built Agartha.

The titular "Claíomh Solais", the sword that sets the plot in motion, is a magical sword that was once wielded by the King Nuada, a king of the Tuatha De Danann. In mythology, the Claíomh Solais was one of the four magical treasures brought to Ireland by the Tuatha de Danann. The other treasures are the Cauldron of the Daghda, the spear of Lugh and the Stone of Fál. The sword itself has parallels to the magical swords of other mythologies throughout Europe, most notably Excalibur of the Arthurian legends.

The Pellucidar Expeditionary Corps: (Lore and inspiration)
One of the key forces in stopping the Fomorians from invading Ireland in this novel is the Pellucidar Expeditionary Corps, an Anglo-American monster hunting organization, inspired by

Edgar Rice Burroughs (see below). In this alternate reality, this organization was founded by the British vampire slayer Johnathan Harker in 1897 (Jonathan is the main protagonist of Bram Stoker's iconic novel and is the one who ultimately kills Dracula).

The name "Pellucidar" was originally the name for Hollow Earth, first given in Edgar Rice Burroughs book "At Earth's Core", published in 1914. I created the P.E.C to make frequent visits to Hollow Earth to fight monsters and prevent them from invading Earth. The central role of P.E.C is to protect both the British Empire and the United States from supernatural and alien threats. By the time of my story, P.E.C is run by Quincy, the son of Johnathan and Mina Harker. Quincy was given his name in memory of an American gunman Quincy Morris who helped the heroes fight Dracula and his minions.

While the P.E.C is my own creation, it is overwhelmingly inspired by the literary culture of the late 19th and early 20th century and even has certain elements of real-life history. As mentioned above, while both Johnathan and Quincy Harker come from Bram Stoker's novel "Dracula", the idea of a secret organization or faction equipped with high tech weapons and gadgets is a common literary trope in Victorian literature. The most famous example of this being Captain Nemo and his massive self-sustaining submarine "Nautilus" from the book "Twenty thousand leagues under the sea" by French author Jules Verne. Some of the advanced technology that P.E.C has at its disposal in my novel is based in actual reality.

For example, underground bases backed with troops and equipment like the P.E.C base Scraw-Fell were actually commonplace in World War 2, most famously the French Maginot Line. Similarly, the first computers, radars, jets and helicopters all came about in this time.

However, in real life, most of these technologies were prototypes. The idea of interdimensional travel and portals was also an increasing theme in science fiction. The name of Scraw-

Fell is inspired by the Belgian graphic novel series "Blake and Mortimer" which had an underground base called "Scaw-Fell". This comic series debuted in the late 1940s after World War 2. A lot of the more mundane gear of P.E.C such as steel helmets, jeeps and semi-automatic rifles is inspired by actual equipment used by both the British and American army during the Second World War and the early Cold War.

The Druids or Society of Saint Patrick (Lore and inspirations)

In the world of the "Claíomh Solais", the Society of Saint Patrick is an indigenous Celtic monster-fighting organization with its own independent hierarchy and a well-trained and well-equipped army. It has its roots in the Christianization of Ireland where the pagan warrior prince, Oisín came back from the mythical land of Tír na Óg. While in the original legend, Oisín withered and died, in this story, he re-established a Christian version of the Fianna in his dying days that would continue to defend Celtic Ireland in the changing times. Ever since the plantations and the conquest of Ireland by Cromwell, the Society of Saint Patrick became a secret society hidden within Ireland's mounds, hoping to end both the rule of the British Empire and the Roman Catholic Church over Ireland. The Society of Saint Patrick names its members Druids, the same name that the pagan priests had in pre–Christian Ireland.

However, the Society of Saint Patrick practices a form of Celtic Christianity, based around the teachings of Saint Columba and Saint Patrick. The Druids, under Lord Donacagh in "The Claíomh Solais" are heavily inspired by Irish Nationalist movements of the early 20th century, particularly the Irish Republican Brotherhood under Patrick Pearse. They also take inspiration from other European ethno-nationalist movements when it comes to their radical extremism. Their uniforms, most notably the Stalhelm helmet, were worn by many European armies including the Swiss, the Irish Free State, Imperial Germany and most infamously the Nazis. The fact that their equipment is mostly German in its appearance is a homage to the strong links that Celtic Irish nationalism had with the Germans. (The Germans often sent weapons and supplies to Irish rebels during the First World War; it was a German composer who helped to organize the first Irish military marching band and it was a German scholar who decoded the Ogham writings).

Lord Donacagh's guards wield broadswords and wear patterned tartans which were similar to those worn by Scottish warriors during the 17th and 18th century. Scotland was another Celtic country who like the Irish had been absorbed into the British Empire. The Irish Celts are also theorized to have conquered Scotland from the Picts. Celtic Christianity was a form of Christianity that was present in the British isles among the Celts in the last years of the Roman Empire. But it was replaced by the Roman Catholic Church in the early middle ages. Lord Donacagh himself was inspired by radical nationalist figures like Patrick Pearse who led the Easter Rising.

Danu, Mother Ireland and Occultic Goddess worship

A key figure within the "Claíomh Solais" is the goddess Danu, a mysterious mother goddess of Ireland who appears to Eric Trent and chooses him to slay Brés. She is also the one who reveals that Eric is a reincarnation of the Tuatha De Danann king Lugh who slew the Fomorian king Balor. But who is Danu? What was she to the Celts? The name Danu comes from the Cycle of invasions where she is credited with bringing the Tuatha De Danann together and sending them to four cities in the North to learn the arts of civilization and magic. Thus, she essentially becomes their mother goddess.

Danu herself is an example of a much more ancient archetype within the European tradition that dates back long before Christianity. In pre-Christian Europe, there is the recurring figure of a mother goddess, a powerful feminine entity gifted with the power of creation and fertility. This being went by many names (i.e. Gaia for the Greeks, Danu for the Irish Celts), a similar figure also appears in non-European mythologies as well. Like many indigenous European Gods, worship of the goddess got increasingly side-lined and marginalized by the Catholic Church's monotheistic religion which put a single (male) God at the centre of cosmology.

However, the archetype of a maternal goddess continued to permeate European culture well into the modern period of guns, the printing press and steam engines. From the late 18th and into the 19th centuries, it became common for a goddess to embody the ideals of the rising nation states. For Britain it was Britannia, for France, Marianne and for America, Columbia while in Ireland, Mother Ireland emerged. During the British occupation of Ireland, Celtic bards and poets often invoked a manifestation of Ireland as a Goddess motivating the men of Ireland to fight for her. This was known as an Aisling poem. One notable example of this was the play "Cathleen Ni Houlihan" which was a joint production between the Anglo-Irish poet and mystic W.B. Yeats and Lady Gregory, the chief organizer of Ireland's Abbey Theatre and a key figure in Ireland's cultural resistance to the British Empire.

Danu in the "Claíomh Solais" was portrayed as having flowing orange-red hair, an emerald dress and icy white skin. These colours were inspired by the Irish tri-colour while the golden harp she is first seen playing was another symbol of Irish nationalism.

Elfland, the gothic novel and the Anglo-Irish influences

The gothic novel was a genre of fiction that emerged primarily in the 18th century in England starting with "The Castle of Otranto" published by Horace Walpole in 1764. It was later popularized by authors such as Anne Radcliffe, Matthew Lewis who wrote "The Monk" in 1796 and most famously Mary Wollstonecraft Shelley who wrote "Frankenstein" in 1818. This genre primarily dealt with supernatural themes and the more carnal aspects of human nature such as the urge to violence. However, in the 19th century the gothic novel began to get mastered by a particular group of people within the British Empire: The Anglo-Irish. From the 17th to early 20th centuries, the Anglo Irish were an aristocratic ruling class that carried out the administration of Ireland when it was ruled by the British Empire. It was a culture mostly descended from the Norman lords that invaded Ireland in the middle ages. Such people were essentially Protestants and imitated the British in every way such as speaking English and adopting English sports such as tennis and cricket.

They ruled the land from great country houses. Many of these houses were eventually burnt down during the Anglo-Irish war in the 1920s.

(Important note: Several key figures including W.B Yeats, that contributed to the Celtic revival while of Anglo-Irish lineage, they weren't just puppets for the British empire, they resisted it themselves).

A particular lineage of Gothic fiction developed among the Anglo Irish. This most famously included "Melmoth the Wanderer" by Charles Maturin in 1820, Sheridan Le Fanu who published his collection "In a Glass Darkly" in 1872, the "Picture of Dorian Grey" by Oscar Wilde in 1890 and most importantly Bram Stoker's Dracula in 1897. Both the Anglo Irish and the Gothic play an important role in shaping "The Claíomh Solais". One of the characters that aids Damien in his quest is Lord Simon Fitzgerald who was of that same Anglo-Irish lineage. Elfland itself, where the Fomorians reside, is a gnarled and twisted land of spikey castles that is rife with gothic imagery. However, Elfland also takes inspiration from the ideas of the faeries living in some form of an otherworld which is a recurring theme in mythology and faery tales. The idea of a barren otherworld full of monsters also draws inspiration from other fantasy works, most notably "Mordor" from J.R.R. Tolkien's "The Lord of the Rings".

Similarly, the Fomorians while coming from Irish mythology also take inspiration from the tales of vampires and undead. The talking crows that serve the main villain Brés are a common trope in European fairy tales, often being associated with witches and pagan Gods.

AUTHOR'S NOTES

First written during the Covid Pandemic in the Summer of 2020, The Claíomh Solais is a peculiar novel to have written, and yet despite it being probably the least relevant novel thematically to our time (due to being set back in the early 20th century), it was probably the most entertaining novel to write. For that reason, it is getting the honour of being the second novel that I shall publish. In contrast to my previous novel Blood and Gears in which I firmly set out to write an epic, The Claíomh Solais had a different origin. It had its roots in fan fiction I had written about both Indiana Jones and the Mummy franchises, both of which were tributes to older pulp adventures written during the early 20th century, hence the novel's setting. Over time, as I wrote the novel, the characters became original and the novel grew into a scenario that was even more dramatic than the stories that inspired it: To summarise the tale, The Claíomh Solais tells the story of Damien O'Laoghaire, an impoverished, hungry but talented youth who lives in the Ireland of 1944, an Ireland that was rich in tradition and belief but also struck by terrible poverty and hanging in an existence in which life was cheap for those lived there.

It is this very poverty that drives a frustrated Damien and his younger brother Seosamh to dig up the titular Claíomh Solais, a magic sword which is powered both by the rays of the sun and the rays of the moon. While this act starts the dynamic between Damien and his boss, Eric Trent whose friendship with Damien is most important for the novel, it is also what awakens the Fomorian King Bres and his faeries to wreak havoc on Ireland. With the entire Irish nation under threat, it is up to Eric, Damien and their allies to fight the Fomorians and save Ireland. Much like the Mummy films, our heroes have to confront monsters which they themselves had unleashed in their obsession for the treasure, thus in some ways such stories can be read as a metaphor for confronting the consequences of your own actions. Thus, from my perspective, The Claíomh Solais is animated by two central motifs: material things and class.

More than the characters themselves, The Claíomh Solais is a novel that is more animated by material things, the most obvious of such commodities is the titular sword, the Claíomh Solais which is both an artefact, an ornament and a weapon. It is also what alerts Bres in the first place and yet it is what will allow the heroes to defeat him. Perhaps the true protagonist is not Eric or Damien but the sword itself, an example of what I personally call the "cursed commodity." This is a term I have made up to refer to a recurring trope in pulp adventure stories, often an ancient object which modern men greedily dig up for their own self-interest only for this to cause spooky and destructive consequences in their lives. One famous example of such a "cursed commodity" is the Arc of the Covenant from Raiders of the Lost Ark, an item which the Nazis try to use for their own ambitions only to be melted by the spirits within in a dramatic display that personally gave me nightmares when I first watched it as a young boy. Cursed commodities also exist in other genres, the One Ring which is the animating force of The Lord of the Rings by J.R.R. Tolkien, would be another famous example of a cursed commodity.

The "cursed commodity" is a perfect mythic motif for Modernity, as especially among Western countries we live in a world in which we think we don't need God, that the world around us can be just reasoned away with science and logic and that the ancient wisdom of our own European forefathers and the indigenous traditions of various non-western cultures around the world are just "old fashioned" or "dated". As it takes place in 1944, The Claíomh Solais represents the coming in of such a modern world into Ireland, but like other examples of pulp stories, it is this materialistic mindset which leads modern men to dig up such ancient artefacts, thus unleashing a terrible evil among the world, an evil which the ancient wisdom of our forefathers knew all too well about.

Despite often having scary consequences, this makes the "Cursed commodity" a strangely hopeful plot device for those who see value in old traditions. It reminds us that there are higher powers and forces which can't just be reasoned out of existence; that you can't just treat the past like archaic garbage and that just living a hedonistic materialistic life is not only insufficient for men, but also potentially quite dangerous. That being said, unlike the Nazis in Indiana Jones, when the heroes of the Claíomh Solais realize the consequences of what they have done, they immediately seek to confront the unleashed evil and set things right. However, the Claíomh Solais is not only item that drives forward the plot. The book is full items and technological devices both real and made up which the heroes use to their advantage in order to fight the Fomorians. While The Claíomh Solais is not the first fantasy book to take place in modernity, it is unique in that modernity and its devices, especially its weapons, are what allow the heroes to defeat the evil faeries and save Ireland.

Thus, unlike many modern fantasy books like Harry Potter which make the heroes rely heavily on magic enchantments and spells, The Claíomh Solais has heroes who rely on all sorts of technological devices from motorcars, telephones, guns and aeroplanes, with even the reactionary warriors of the Society of Saint Patrick having an array of fictional yet technologically advanced machines such as armoured zeppelins. In fact, think of any major technological device that appeared in the 19th or 20th century and it probably gets at least a mention in the novel. (That even includes computers and helicopters) While some of the technology is anachronistic it nevertheless reinforces the fact that the world of The Claíomh Solais is a world of objects and devices.

But despite some of the dangers that such materialism can promote, The Claíomh Solais comes off as a very pro-modernity novel as it is through the use of modern machinery and devices that the heroes are able to defeat the Fomorian army, but that is not the only benefit that the modern world can bring to most of humanity. This brings us to our second motif of the novel, which is class, a motif that is unavoidable in any representation of early 20th century Ireland as the brute reality is that most people living in Ireland, especially those of the working class lived harsh brutal lives and had to endure without the material comforts that we modern men take for granted. Modern westerners, (especially environmentalists) often forget just how brutal life was before modern industrialisation, for in that era, men worked under harsh conditions and died from illnesses that are easily treatable today while women died from childbirth all too often. It was into such a world that Damien was born A quintessential working-class hero, Damien's desire for material wealth comes not from the sin of greed but rather a desperate desire to escape the cruel world he and his fellow villagers were born into.

Far from being the noble peasant fantasized by revivalists such as W.B. Yeats, Damien has more in common with Maguire, the hardened and frustrated hero of Patrick Kavanagh's poetic masterpiece The Great Hunger. This makes him the foil for his boss and mentor Eric Trent, who is on surface level, a wealthy English squire who embodies the chivalric ideals of the European aristocrat. Being a supernatural figure who is essentially chosen by the Irish goddess to fight Bres, Eric is the more familiar protagonist to fantasy readers, a chosen aristocratic hero who has to fight evil. If Damien parallel's Kavanagh's Maguire, then Eric parallels the knightly heroes of Lord Alfred Tennyson. Eric is the older and more scholarly figure while Damien is more practical, having learnt to think on his feet. Despite these differences, Eric and Damien are strongly linked.

Instead of the class conflict that Marxists have tried to instigate through the 19th, 20th and 21st centuries, The Claíomh Solais treats the alliance between Tennyson's knight and Kavanagh's underdog as a proper camaraderie that is hierarchal by nature but also built on a mutual respect that the two develop for each other. With the help of other allies, they are able to save Ireland. As Damien catches a glimpse of the other ranks of Irish society, he comes to appreciate his home village more, especially after it has been threatened by the Fomorians. He grows from wanting nothing to do with his hometown to developing a desire to protect and improve it so that it can survive. He learns the mentality of "noblesse oblige" in which the powerful and affluent have a duty to protect those who are more vulnerable. In return, and with mutual respect, they work together to create a more civilized world. This sentiment is, as far as I am concerned, a healthier mentality than either violent depravity of revolutions like the French and Russian revolutions or the harsh domineering attitudes of ruling classes whose cruelty sows the seeds for the revolutionary sentiment.

Along with the motifs of class and commodities, The Claíomh Solais is a story of what is essentially the clash of two different worlds: A world of religion, superstition and simplicity (represented by the Fomorians and the Irish peasantry) and a world of abundance, technology and scientific reason (represented by both the Irish state and the Anglo-American organisation the Pellucidar Expeditionary Corps), one is spiritually rich and materialistically sparse while the other is materialistically rich and spiritually sparse.

It is between these two mentalities that our hero Damien and to an extent, the Irish as a whole must find a balance between, hopefully coming to a healthy balance of appreciating the values of both the spiritual and the material. His mentor, Eric has already achieved that balance.

To finish off these notes, I would like to personally mount a defence of the Irish Free State which forms the backdrop of this novel and into which Damien was born. While not portrayed as a pleasant world to live in in The Claíomh Solais, it is nevertheless a force of good and manly valour as it uses its limited resources to defend its people from the Fomorians. In real life, the Irish nation did make terrible mistakes with tragic consequences (most notably giving too much power to the Irish clergy who certainly abused to those in their care and got away it) and such errors should not be forgotten given how many lives they ruined.

But at the same time, I think the establishment of the Irish state was a heroic venture in of itself. Dealing with the consequences of British colonization even after it became independent, the new Irish state had to deal with all sorts of adversities from the start including the fact that the North was still under British control; the onset of the Great Depression and dangerous ideologies such as Marxism and Fascism as well as the violence of the Second World War. Like Damien, many people lived in poverty through the state's early years but by the end of the 20th century, the Irish Republic had managed to turn a battered and impoverished colony (One that endured a great Famine) into one of the most stable democracies of the Western world. (A Republic which has notably not engaged in acts of imperialism or the forced displacement of other peoples). In conclusion, Damien and the Fomorians he fights may be fictional but Irish heroism certainly is not.

ACKNOWLEDGEMENT

I would like to thank everyone, especially my family who has supported me in the completion and publication of my book.

Finally, I would like to thank the Inkslingers from the Irish Writers center for their support and advice when it comes not just to publishing this novel, but the novels that are to come.

ABOUT THE AUTHOR

Declan Cosson

Declan Cosson was born in Paris, France in 1999. He moved to Ireland in 2001 where he has lived ever since.
He attended Hollypark school between 2005 and 2012. He then attended Clonkeen College between 2012 and 2018 and studied English, Media and Cultural Studies in IADT in Dun Laoghaire between 2018 and 2022.

Declan started writing as early as fifteen years old and has been writing ever since. Currently he is 23 years old. During his time in Clonkeen, he contributed short stories to the Clonkeen Anthology and also contributed short stories to Ink slinger's anthology at the Irish Writer's centre. In 2021, he published a short story collection called the "Collection of the Yearly Strange" and published his first novel "Blood and Gears" in 2023. The Claíomh Solais is his latest publication.

BOOKS BY THIS AUTHOR

Blood And Gears

In the grim dark future of the 24th century, the harsh, regimented and pragmatic state of Terra has been trapped in what seems like a forever war against robotic machines which were created to end World War Three. Drafted into its superhuman army, the Legion, nineteen year old Zach Harker is paired with the battle hardened "Alpha Squad" or "Team Orca", a team of commandos who are thrown into the most dangerous situations in battle.

As he navigates the brutal world of the human-machine war, Zach finds his virtues and principles put to the test, often having to choose between the values of his nation, and that of his instinct.

BOOKS BY THIS AUTHOR

Collection Of The Yearly Strange

The Collection of the Yearly Strange is a short story collection that details terrifying encounters throughout history into the future. These tales will take you from the gas lit streets of early 20th century London to the Mid Western US at the height of the Cold War and then towards the deepest depths of the Atlantic Ocean and even to the furthest reaches of the Alpha Centauri. Along the way, you will meet a plethora of creatures ranging from heroic humans to robotic and insectoid monstrosities to even alien invaders ready to abduct.

Though the tools, culture and weapons may change throughout history, one constant in these tales remains. And that is that there is always something that goes bump in the night when you least expect it. Because of that these tales are not for the faint hearted.